D1507611

THE LOST LEGEND
of the First Christmas

THE LOST LEGEND
of the First Christmas

BOOK ONE
OF THE

Lost Legend Trilogy

Written & Illustrated By

J.L. *Hardesty*

Cover Painting By
Richard L. Marks

PUBLISHED BY

AMPELOS PRESS

The Lost Legend of the First Christmas
Copyright © 1999 Jo Hardesty Lauter

First Edition

ISBN 0-9661305-1-0

Cover Painting by Richard L. Marks
Illustrations by J. L. Hardesty
Cover and Text Design
by Images Unlimited

Published by:
Ampelos Press
Drexel Hill, Pennsylvania
Colorado Office
P.O. Box 773632
Steamboat Springs
Colorado 80477

Printed in Hong Kong
by Pacific Rim International Printing, Los Angeles, CA

To the horses . . .
those glorious creatures God sent
to carry us on our journey home,
to Him.

Special Thanks
to my husband, Jim Lauter,
for his love and belief in my writing.

~

To my dear friend and editor,
Marlene Bagnull,
for her enormous, unselfish,
utterly invaluable
help and encouragement.

~

To the angel known
as Michele, sent by God
to turn our dreams into reality.

PROLOGUE

From the days of long ago a story of immense consequence has been handed down, generation to generation. It is the account of a boy of great courage and two horses of great heart who, together, encountered the Christ Child and through Him took part in the greatest story ever told.

This is a tale recounted for centuries around night fires all across the land from Marrakesh to Ceylon, from Rome to South Africa, from the mountain tops of Peru to the grassy plains of the brave land to the North—and beyond. A lengthy narrative, the story was traditionally shared during the twelve nights that precede the blessed celebration of Christ's birth, the anniversary known as Christmas.

Throughout the ages, no culture in which there were horsemen was without its carrier of the legend, which lived always in the hearts and the minds of the old ones—the keepers of the wisdom—until the old ones and their ways began to die out. And even then, the story was miraculously preserved.

Recorded by the trembling hand of a dying elder of a Native North American people who valued the horse above all other earthly treasures, it was hidden away to be found many generations later by a child of the Americas who would understand and once again pass the legend on.

The child grew old, as children do, and entrusted to me this tale it is now my responsibility to tell.

CHAPTER
One

Our story begins some two thousand years ago, when a mighty emperor known as Caesar Augustus ruled over all of the vast Roman Empire; and beneath him, a cruel king called Herod governed the country then named Judea. During that time, there lived an elite sect of astronomers who studied the skies in search of wisdom—the essence of their quest, an understanding of the One God whom they believed to be the true ruler of all the earth and the nations upon it.

These men, known as the Magi, or Wise Men, were often sought by kings such as Herod for their insight and knowledge. On other occasions, the authority-mad rulers had the Wise Men hunted down and killed for fear of the implied power of their genius.

Among the most brilliant of the Magi was a tall, handsome man called Archanus. It is with this Wise Man and his son, Michael, that our story unfolds.

It was the time of day when the long shadows of evening at last lay down to await the dawn. The late summer sun was slipping beneath the horizon and only its glow illuminated the western sky. The night began its gentle symphony as the creatures of the day sought refuge from the encroaching darkness, the chirping of crickets filling the calm wherein the day birds no longer sang.

High up on a gently sloping hillside Archanus and Michael sat, silently watching the sun surrender to the dusk. They marveled at the speed with which the golden orb descended. They were awed by the changing moods and colors that pulsed within the broad bank of fugitive clouds behind which the sun did its last dance of the day. Then there was only darkness.

A cloak of fear settled heavily over the companions as they awaited the arrival of the stars that would fill and decorate the night sky. Time seemed to stop. Humans and horses were taken captive by a tense stillness. Eyes and ears strained to detect the slightest sign of approaching danger. For a time, no light or sound relieved the dark hush until, as if by magic, a blanket of stars appeared and the glow of the quarter moon breached the twilight.

"What will they tell you tonight?" Michael asked, relieved by the soft illumination and glad to break the strained silence. "The stars, I mean—where will they lead us?"

Archanus looked down at the handsome boy beside him. At twelve, the dark-haired, blue-eyed youngster was the image of his mother, a likeness that brought to the father alternating surges of joy and sorrow.

"To your mother's people," Archanus answered. "The stars lead us to your mother's people."

"And then?"

"We'll travel with the horsemen for a while. Then I must continue my journey alone."

"Why can't I go with you?" The boy's voice trembled with fear and longing.

"It's not safe. You know that," Archanus reminded himself as well as his son. "Until I am no longer in danger, you will be better off without me."

"But where will you go?"

"I don't know for certain. Wherever I travel, though, I'll continue my quest."

"Will we really meet again—you and my mother and I?"

"Yes, we shall." Archanus placed a strong arm around his son and pulled the boy close. "When we have completed our sojourns through the earth, we'll join your mother at the throne of God."

"Until then?"

"We must have courage and do our best to carry out the work He has for us to do."

"What will that work be?"

"I believe each of us will be charged with an assignment of great importance, Beyond that, I do not know."

"What kind of assignment?" the boy asked.

"I'm not certain. I just sense God's presence in the events that have led us here. I don't think He would have saved us if He did not have something important for us to accomplish. We will know in God's time." Archanus paused. "Now you must rest."

"And you?"

"I dare not sleep until we meet with the horsemen. Someone must stand watch."

Archanus sat upright, his back against a large rock that offered shelter from the night breeze. Remaining alert, the Wise Man allowed his mind to wander back to the city and the nightmarish drama that brought him and his son to this juncture in their lives.

"How rapidly life changes," he thought. It had been only a fortnight since Junia's passing. Yet, since then, it seemed as though nearly a lifetime had transpired. In sad reflection, Archanus could scarcely bear to think of the confined space where his dear wife had spent her last days. Too late he understood how Junia must have longed for the sweet light that lingered beyond the shadowed lane onto which their only door opened. "Junia, my love." Archanus' whisper caught on a sob. "How could I have taken you from the life you cherished? The city was never a good place for you. You must have felt like a prisoner within those walls."

The Wise Man recalled with regret the turning point three years earlier when he and Junia agreed to go to the city. Each had been visited in dreams by an angel calling Archanus into the service of the One God.

"You must go to the place where Hebrew scholars and Magi will be gathered," explained the angel. "There you will learn about the Messiah."

"Is this the One many believe will arrive soon to save the world?" Archanus asked the angel.

"It is He."

"We will do the angel's bidding," said Junia when the couple discussed their dreams the following morning.

"I cannot ask you to make this sacrifice."

"It is a blessing, my husband. What good is a life that cannot be given in love?"

"How prophetic were those words," Archanus thought now. "You could not have known, my dearest love, that you would, in truth, give your life."

A loving and considerate man, Archanus never meant to cause suffering for his family. In the new surroundings, though, he had become consumed by his quest for knowledge. Focused on his studies, he didn't see how the nomadic spirits of his wife and son were withering in the heavy closeness of city life.

Now Archanus cursed himself for the awful decision that had surely taken Junia from him, and from Michael. "How could I have been so selfish?" he asked the glistening sky, remembering a promise made too late. "I cannot ask you to suffer this any longer," he had told Junia. "We'll return to your people and the horses you love. I'll learn everything else I need to know from the messages God sends through the stars and from men of wisdom we meet in our travels. I do not need my kinsmen as you need your freedom."

That pledge could not be fulfilled. Junia was one of the first fatalities of a terrible sickness that swept the city. Taking another kind of journey, the young wife and mother went to be with her God, leaving behind forever her joys and her sorrows.

"Was it your unhappiness that really took you and not the disease?" Archanus spoke as though something of Junia lingered nearby. "Will my misery take me to your side? And why didn't our God let me fall to the Roman's sword?" With these questions, the grieving man was at last transported to the events that made him a fugitive . . .

The afternoon air was heavy and still. No breeze relieved the stifling heat. The street soldiers argued among themselves as they followed slivers of shade from building to building. Women hid in their stuffy houses, afraid to be seen and rudely accosted by the barbarians who roamed their town. Even the normally talkative merchants kept to themselves, reluctant to cause any annoyance that might incite their cruel oppressors to violence.

From the marketplace at the hub of the community, narrow corridors fanned out like the spokes of a wheel. On each side of the dim foot paths, private households huddled together, separated only by common mud-brick walls. Single access doors at the center of each home broke the monotony of the long, windowless facades. Flat rooftops, accessed by shared stairways, provided open air living and working spaces.

There were three rooms in Archanus' and Junia's small house. At the front was the area in which meals were prepared and eaten. To the rear were the sleeping quarters. Archanus paced the floor in the front room, struggling with a decision he knew he must make. Now that Junia was gone, should he and his son remain in the city? Or should they rejoin Junia's people?

There was still much to learn in this place, but Michael must be considered. It was bad enough with Junia there to keep her son company. Without her, the boy seemed to have retreated to some inaccessible place within himself. Archanus knew that his son's heart ached with the grief of a loss his mind refused to comprehend. What the father didn't know was how he could help.

"Talk to him." Archanus looked around for the source of the gentle admonition, but no one was there.

"Go to him. He's waiting." This time, the Wise Man felt, rather than heard the message.

Finally, in response, Archanus pulled aside the drape at the entrance to Michael's sleeping chamber. The boy sat dejectedly on his cot, waiting, it seemed, but for what?

Archanus cleared his throat, searching for just the right words.

"Listen," Michael whispered. "Can you hear them?"

Concentrating on what he would say, Archanus had

not heard the approach of the three Roman soldiers who stood, at that moment, arguing just outside the door.

"What will we do?" Michael asked, alarm replacing the sadness in his eyes.

"We wait. The Merciful God surely sees our needs."

"You, inside!" yelled one of the men. "Come out!"

"Why do you not go in and drag them out?" A second man spoke in a scornful tone. "You're always bragging about your great size and strength. What do you fear?"

"You know this one is under the Tribune Zadoc's protection," the first man replied.

"Zadoc is not here," snarled another, "and Tabeel has ordered us to dispatch this Magi forthwith!"

"Are you so afraid of Zadoc that you are willing to disobey Tabeel?" mocked the third soldier.

"Tabeel is not our superior officer. He is merely the proconsul of this city."

"But he has money to pay for our services!" the first soldier reminded his companions.

"What is the disturbance?" a newcomer demanded.

Archanus recognized the fourth voice as that of Marcus, the eldest member of the Magi.

"We have come to arrest the man of your sect who is responsible for the death of the proconsul's wife," said one of the soldiers. "You will do well to take your leave, old man."

But the elder Magi would not be brushed aside so easily. When the first soldier moved toward the door to Archanus' dwelling, Marcus stepped between the Roman and his target.

"This man has done no wrong," Marcus said calmly. "He and his wife only tried to help when they encountered those in need."

"Your friend brought a curse down upon us," spat the soldier who appeared to be in charge. "He will die for his crimes."

Just as Archanus opened the door and stepped out to protect his friend, one of the Romans grabbed the elder and roughly shoved him out of the way.

"Your business is with me." Archanus spoke with the natural authority possessed by men of his immense stature. "Let Marcus alone."

"Not now," barked the leader. "The old man has interfered. Now he too will die."

With no thought for his own safety, Archanus fell upon the leader and wrestled him to the ground. None of the soldiers were as large and powerful as was Archanus. But there were three of them, and they had weapons. At first, the Wise Man was able to hold his own because of his superior strength, but after a time, he began to succumb.

Marcus knelt beside Michael, his eyes raised to the heavens, his voice resonant as he prayed to the One God for help in this time of great need.

Suddenly, one of the soldiers crashed to the ground, his arms raised to cover his face and head as if to protect himself from a barrage of blows.

Archanus was on his back beneath the two remaining soldiers who were trying vainly to subdue him. All at once, first one and then the other of the assailants appeared to be roughly jerked off of Archanus and thrown through the air. One body landed in a crumpled heap some twenty feet away. The other slammed against the wall across from Archanus' door before landing face down on the dusty pathway.

Horrified by the bizarrely contorted bodies of the fallen soldiers, the Wise Men and the boy could only stare in silent relief as the third leapt to his feet and ran away as fast as his trembling legs would carry him.

In the wake of the near disaster, Archanus and Marcus fell to their knees, offering up words of thanks and praise to the One God. For long moments, they remained thus, their heads bowed in reverence and gratitude.

Silently, Michael observed the sacred ritual, his eyes a mirror of confusion. When the Wise Men rose at last, Archanus reached out to his son. "We must gather our things and escape at once."

"But Father, I do not understand."

"It is no longer safe for us here. The soldiers will return with many others."

"No, that is not what I mean. I do not understand what happened. I saw the soldiers falling but no one touched them. There were only the three of us . . . and we were unarmed—"

"Ah, so it would appear," interjected Marcus with a gentle smile. "Some things, though, are not as they seem."

"We have read in the ancient scrolls that God will send his angels to deliver His people in times of great need," Archanus explained.

"Angels?" questioned Michael, "I saw no angels."

"Sometimes we cannot see those who come to save us," said Archanus. "Nonetheless, they are there . . . angels sent by God to protect us."

"This is all very strange to me," said Michael, shaking his head and looking from his father to their friend.

"You will see many things far stranger in the days ahead," said the elder Magi, not knowing then how much truth there was in those simple words.

CHAPTER
Two

In the land of his dreams, Michael traveled beside his father. In spirit, each relived his part, their senses elevated by an unseen guide.

In the shelter of the rock where his father stood guard, Michael dreamed of the meeting that took place a few days after the soldiers' attack. Standing watch near the mouth of the cave where the fugitives had hidden since the skirmish, the boy listened while Archanus and other members of the Magi discussed the trouble that faced them. It was common for the Magi and other scholars to gather for studious discourse about the imminent coming of the Jews' prophesied Savior. This was not, however, an ordinary occasion. This day the air was alive with tension, the setting unfamiliar, and the conversation far from usual.

"We cannot keep speculating," Michael heard his father say. "We must seek the Source. How can we proceed without heavenly guidance?"

"Have we not angered the One God?" Michael recognized the voice of Malachi, a small, dark man who studied with his father.

"There has been no answer to our prayers," a second Magi interrupted. "You, of all people, Archanus, should realize that we have been forsaken."

"You have brought disfavor upon us and made our lives more dangerous than ever," another accused.

"Now we cannot even leave the city," Malachi spoke again. "Travel is too perilous. The soldiers don't care which of us they capture in their efforts to find you."

"We'll never see the coming of the Savior, thanks to you." Kiros, the earlier accuser, snarled.

"My friends, please." The patient entreaty came from Marcus. "Archanus has done nothing that any man of love and courage would not have done. He only meant to protect me."

At the cave's entrance, a giant of a man in the garb of a Roman soldier tousled Michael's hair affectionately and caught the boy up in a powerful embrace. Like Archanus, the Tribune, Zadoc, was a handsome young man. His enormous stature and exceptional intelligence enabled him to ascend to a position of high command much earlier in life than was common.

"Come," said Zadoc to the boy who was as dear to him as a son. "My men will stand guard. You're a part of this. You need to hear what's being discussed."

"What is happening here?" The Tribune spoke with rough authority as he entered the meeting chamber.

"Zadoc!" Archanus rose from his place and grasped

the hand of the newcomer. "Thank God you have returned. There has been chaos in the streets without you."

The giant glanced around the room appraising his audience. His gaze rested on the sullen Malachi who looked furtively away from the all-seeing eyes of the imposing Roman. Michael knew that these two men distrusted one another. He remembered how Zadoc had once described Malachi as a small man in more ways than one—a man governed by fear.

"Malachi pretends to be suspicious of me because I am half Hebrew by descent and a Roman soldier by choice," Zadoc had laughed. "But the truth is, he knows that I am aware of his deceit."

"Send the boy away." Malachi, squirming under Zadoc's hard assessment, spoke into the unforgiving hush. "He's too young to be a part of this."

Archanus stepped to Michael's side and put an arm around the boy. But it was Zadoc who spoke.

"He is more a man than you will ever be. He will stay—and his presence will be welcomed."

Michael recalled how the Magi had come to know Zadoc when the powerful soldier saved Marcus from a drunken mob. Inevitably, the boy's heart reached out to his beloved mother, who was the first of the Magi's women to welcome the Tribune into her home.

"I am sorry, my friends." Zadoc spoke again, his words drawing Michael from thoughts of Junia. "I did not plan to be gone so long," the big soldier said, crossing the cavern, then stopping beside Marcus. "What has happened?" he asked, looking to the elder for explanation. "I know part of the story from my men. But I do not know everything that went on, or why."

"Some of Herod's mob tried to arrest Archanus," little Malachi spat, not giving Marcus a chance to respond.

"Why couldn't Archanus just surrender?" snapped Kiros. "Sometimes we have to make sacrifices for the cause—"

"It's not so easy for most of us to abandon our friends and family," another said firmly.

"Be still," Zadoc ordered. "I have asked Marcus to explain. Let him speak."

The old man took a moment, seeming to put his thoughts in order. Then, beginning with Junia's passing, he described the events that led up to the current predicament.

"Since the soldiers tried to arrest Archanus, we have been in hiding." Marcus completed his explanation. "We all came together this afternoon to plan our permanent escapes from the dangerous situation we share and to bid one another a last farewell."

Another silence fell over the assembly. Every fearful eye in the room was on Zadoc, who spoke, finally, with his accustomed command. "Kiros and Malachi, you must depart at once. The soldiers will be at rest or in the tavern retreating from the afternoon heat. Go to the cave on the other side of the village and wait there. You will be taken out of the area after nightfall. Do not stop anywhere along the way. Speak to no one or you will be the first of this company to perish."

The two men looked to one another for support then sneaked wary glances around the room. "Why are we being singled out?" Kiros whined.

"Because you have no families to collect before your departure," Zadoc answered reasonably. "Do you not agree that yours will be the simplest escape and that someone of your creed must be saved?"

"Yes, yes of course," the conspirators spoke at once and, without a backward glance, took their leave.

"Now," Zadoc continued, "each of you must return to your homes. Gather what belongings you can easily carry and wait for nightfall. When the soldiers sleep, I will come to you separately and men I trust will escort you and your families to safety."

"How will you manage?" one of the Wise Men asked. "There are fifteen of us, plus our families, besides Kiros and Malachi."

"Please, have a little faith in your God," Zadoc said. "He will save you. I am only His messenger, but I will do His bidding well."

When everyone except Marcus, Archanus, Michael, and Zadoc had departed, the elder spoke. "I am too old to travel, my friends. You must leave me behind."

"No!" Archanus cried. "We cannot abandon you to the barbarians who will again be in control while Zadoc is away!"

"Nor will we," Zadoc spoke calmly. "Marcus will have safe harbor in my home while my men and I take the rest of you away from here. Once that is accomplished, I will deliver Marcus to his new home."

"Do not despair," he added gently. "First, we must save you and your son. But what still bothers you? I see a question in your eyes."

"I am sorry—" Archanus began hesitantly.

"Perhaps I have answers for your questions." The Tribune smiled, hoping to put his friend's mind at ease.

"Well, I was wondering, how is it that you find us in the cave?"

"I have had men watching you the entire time that I was away. They were not dressed as soldiers and were able to blend rather well into their surroundings. They saw what happened, and they followed you when you made your hasty retreat. They were instructed not to expose themselves to you or to the soldiers. Had your lives truly been in peril, however, my men would have disobeyed this order to save you. Now, what else do you want to know?"

Archanus shook his head. "You amaze me, my friend. You seem always to think of everything. Why did you send Malachi and Kiros away as you did? The reason you gave was surely valid, but perhaps not the real one."

"Those two cannot be trusted," Zadoc said simply. "Given the chance, they would betray us all. They can only be controlled by fear for their lives. You see, my friends, even among your own there is treachery. My men will escort them to a far land, where none of us is likely to be harmed by their duplicity."

Leaning back against the rock, the exhausted Archanus traveled beside his sleeping son on memory's highway. With terrible sorrow he recalled the evening following that last meeting of the Magi when he sat in the cave awaiting the Tribune's return.

For the first time since his wife's passing, Archanus began to face the reality that Junia was truly gone. In final farewell, he sang softly a song of his childhood, a prayer for the safe passage of Junia's spirit into the realm of God's everlasting peace. When his song was ended, the Wise Man looked to the future. Praying for the safety of his son and for the healing of the boy's broken heart, he wished and asked nothing at all for himself.

While Archanus was still in prayer, the light of a flickering candle in the passageway signaled Zadoc's arrival.

"We must depart, my friend." The Tribune spoke gently, but without preamble. "Kiros and Malachi have already made good their betrayal and what they believe to be their own escape."

Archanus looked up at his friend, and his eyes reflected the awful sorrow that overflowed from his heart. The Wise Man knew the Tribune could offer no comfort. It was simply impossible to hide his anguish any longer.

No further words passed between the friends as they roused Michael from his sleep, gathered the travelers' few belongings, and left the cave to begin their perilous expedition. Day and night they journeyed. Stopping only to give the horses feed and rest, they conversed little as they trekked through a land devoid of human occupation. Now and then Zadoc rode ahead to scout the trail then returned to guard his charges, apparently tireless and ever alert.

As night fell on the seventh day, the companions came under attack. From the North, a terrible hoard of thieves swooped down. Shouting obscenely and brandishing all manner of weaponry, the assailants' aim was to unseat the riders and to steal their fine horses.

Archanus began at once to pray. "Dear Lord," he called, "What will it be, this time? Your magic, or my own?"

As if in answer, a fierce wind suddenly engulfed the desert pirates and their unsteady mounts. The marauders cursed in frustration as their flashing swords bounced ineffectively off of targets that should have been easily breached.

Unarmed, Archanus and Michael watched in awe as three of their attackers were flung into the chasm that fell away from the steep trail. Then, with no more than a few quick thrusts of his sword, Zadoc dispatched the remaining criminals.

"What will become of the poor creatures?" Michael asked, watching sadly as the thieves' gaunt horses fled.

"They're free now," Archanus answered, proud of the concern for the animals that had been instilled in Michael by his mother. "There's good water and a grassy meadow not far from here. They'll find their way, and they're far better off than they were in the hands of those evil men."

That night, Archanus and Zadoc, unable to sleep, sat gazing into the darkness.

"Could you feel the protection?" Archanus asked.

"Yes." Zadoc smiled. "How did you do that? Was it some sort of magic?"

"No," Archanus said. "Just prayer . . . I called to God for help. And He sent His angels to our rescue."

"Just as He did when Marcus prayed for your deliverance in the city," Zadoc said.

"Yes—" Archanus smiled ironically. "And I too first thought of magic when Marcus summoned the angels. Why, I wonder, is it so much easier for all of us to believe in magic than in God's awesome power?"

"I don't know," Zadoc answered. "But I wish my faith could be as strong as yours."

"Mine is not as great as I would like it to be," said the Wise Man. "In fact, I had precious little faith until Junia came into my life. She taught me how small our magic is when compared to the dominion of the One God—"

"She is well and happy now," Zadoc said. "It is you who taught me this truth which you must now embrace."

"Why, Zadoc?" Archanus asked, his eyes dark with grief. "Why did the God she loved so well take her from us? Twice now, He has sent his angels to protect Michael and me. Why didn't he send them to cure Junia?"

"Perhaps He loved her too much to let her suffer this mortal soil any longer." Zadoc rested a gentle hand on his friend's shoulder. "Maybe she could not be a part of what lies ahead for you and your son . . . Someday you will know. For now, we can only go and do God's bidding and await the understanding He will eventually give us."

Two days later, the Tribune prepared to depart. "I know you stayed longer than you should have because you feared for our safety," Archanus said, gripping Zadoc's hand.

"Yes, a little." The guardian smiled. "I can only leave now because I finally understand the extent of the angelic protection you have been given."

Archanus released his friend's hand and squared his broad shoulders.

"Until we meet again, may your God be with us all," Zadoc said, taking the reins from Michael who stood patiently holding the Tribune's horse.

"He is our God," Archanus said. "You are as much under His protection as are we."

"Yes, I think this is so," Zadoc said softly. "Soon after Junia first invited me into your home, she told me that I too am a child of this Almighty God. I thought she was only being kind. I know, now, that she spoke the truth."

"When will we meet again?" Michael asked, patting the horse's neck, making a show of adjusting the saddle so that the two older men would not see the shining tears in his eyes.

"Only the One God knows," Zadoc replied, placing a hand on Michael's shoulder and turning the boy into his strong embrace. "He will tell us what we are to do—and one day He will bring us together again. Until then, we must follow the paths of His guiding. This too your father has taught me," the Tribune said, saluting his friends as he mounted his horse and turned to ride away.

Memories and dreams . . . and a final farewell. The essence of the wife, the mother, would linger no more. On her loved ones' shared and separate journeys, she had been their guide. The mother had succeeded in drawing her husband and son closer together than they had ever been before. Through this dark night of their souls, Junia had led her man and her boy to the sure understanding that, through them, her courageous heart would, indeed, go on.

CHAPTER
Three

Ahead of the dawn, with the night's revelations behind him, Archanus prepared for the day. Not wishing to disturb his son, the Magi went quietly about the business of tending to the horses, lighting a morning fire, and laying out a small meal.

These simple chores completed, he sat down beside his son and waited. Lovingly, Archanus watched the slight rise and fall of the warm rugs that covered the sleeping boy. A lock of dark hair fell across Michael's forehead nearly touching the long, thick lashes that fluttered, now and then.

"How can I leave you?" the father barely whispered, reaching out to touch his sleeping son, taking comfort in the small intimacy.

"Is it time to go?" the boy asked, rubbing his sleepy eyes, awakening though his father had not meant to disturb him.

On the eastern horizon the sky was aglow. The previous night's blanket of stars had retreated at the intrusion of dawn. The moon slipped behind the hills in the west. Only the bright morning star was still visible in the heavens. And soon, as quickly as it had descended on the night before, the fiery sun would begin its ascent into the warming sky.

"Morning is here," Archanus said, rising. "I suppose we should get started. We have a long journey ahead of us."

Michael arose without further urging. He rolled up his sleeping rugs and secured them with a leather thong, then walked down to the stream that wound along the foot of the hill.

Archanus had tethered the horses to a nearby tree where they could nibble on the lush grasses that grew up along the creek and drink their fill before beginning the day's travels. As his mother had taught him, Michael thought of the horses first, unconcerned with his own needs until he was sure these faithful servants were well and satisfied.

So that he wouldn't startle them, Michael talked to the animals as he came near. "I hope you had a good night's rest," he said, as though he were talking to a pair of human companions. "Our path could be difficult today."

The bay gelding, who was called Eleuzis, had served Michael's mother well since before the boy's birth. Now the horse looked up from his grazing and greeted his young friend with a low, rumbling nicker. Not to be outdone, the gray, Spartan, added his greeting. Both horses reached their warm noses toward Michael, looking for treats, knowing that deep in his pockets their caretaker always carried little cakes of grain sweetened with honey and molasses. But there were no sweets this morning. Michael's supply had run out.

The boy wanted to explain to the horses that some things change when you're forced to run for your very life. He wanted to make these loyal creatures understand what he could not, that the One God had summoned his mother home and that his father was being hunted by the Romans. As Michael wrestled with the apparent injustice of these events, both horses nudged at him impatiently. A deep sadness settled over the young horseman as he realized that there was no way he could communicate these complex events to the animals.

Murmuring gently, his tone conveying what his words could not, Michael began his routine examination of the horses. First he patted the bay's long neck, then ran his hand gently down the horse's front legs, feeling for swelling or heat that might need attention. He continued, touching softly every inch of each horse, from head to heel. It took only a few moments to complete his inspection and to satisfy himself that both horses were in

good health. It was a ceremony his mother had performed every day of Michael's life, a ritual the boy inherited along with Eleuzis.

"I'll be back soon," Michael said, again patting each of the horses and turning to make his way back up the hill to rejoin his father.

Watching his son's interaction with the horses, Archanus marveled again at the connection between these animals and the people of Junia's blood. Since his first encounter with the horsemen many years earlier, Archanus had remained amazed at the way these people so quietly and calmly handled the big animals that, for most other humans, could be so difficult.

Since virtually every member of Junia's tribe dealt fearlessly with these great four-legged enigmas, Archanus at first thought that perhaps the horses of this tribe were a different sort, less fractious, less prone to skittishness and wayward behavior than others of their kind. But soon enough, he learned that this was not the case. His own first efforts to handle and then to ride Spartan, a wedding gift to him from Junia's parents, were almost disastrous.

Even now, Archanus blanched with embarrassment at the memories of too many unceremonious departures from Spartan's back and the painful landings that inevitably followed. The Magi's only relief from total humiliation was the simple fact that he wasn't alone in his plight.

It was customary for the Roman soldiers who could master the art of horsemanship to purchase their horses from Junia's tribe. The battles that ensued between horse and man on the occasions of these acquisitions were legendary. Every horse soldier had to prove his grit each time he acquired a new mount. If any man showed cruelty to the animals, that man was branded a coward and demoted back to the infantry.

Twice a year, a group of Roman soldiers would arrive at the horsemen's camp, choose their new mounts from the selection offered, then spend a few days becoming acquainted with the animals. Spectacular competitions were held during these rendezvous.

The soldier who showed the most patience and courage in his efforts to stay aboard the wildly bucking animals received the grand prize of an additional mount from the horsemen. The soldier who rode the wildest horse for the longest time received a prize of gold coins from his companions.

At the end of every such event, only a few of the dozens of men who participated in these ancient rodeos rode away aboard a horse. The lion's share of the contenders always remained afoot, having been thoroughly bested by the horses. Those who became horse soldiers in that day of the Roman infantry were revered by all for their unique and remarkable accomplishments.

Fortunately for Archanus and his new bride, one such encounter took place shortly after Archanus' receipt of the dubious gift called Spartan. Seeing the stalwart soldiers being humbled by the horses, as he had been, reduced Archanus' shame and encouraged him to remain steadfast in his attempts to conquer the wild and wily Spartan.

Memories continued to assault the Wise Man as he watched his son on this fair morning. Among the most poignant of those recollections was a conversation with Junia in which Archanus had suggested that if the horse were predisposed to serving all the peoples of the world as they were the horsemen, human communication, travel, and commerce would be improved beyond imagination. He couldn't help but smile now, as he thought of Junia's quick and sure response.

"The average human," she said, "is far too thoughtless and greedy to be entrusted with the care of these fine creatures. We can only hope that if God ever decides to alter the nature of the horse, He will first improve the character of the humans He allows the horse to serve."

Roused from his reminiscing when Michael appeared, Archanus wondered how long the boy had been standing before him.

"Are you hungry?" the man asked, hastening to cover his embarrassment.

"Starved," smiled the boy, rubbing his stomach.

"Come and eat, then. We still have plenty and soon we'll come to another encampment where we can trade for more provisions."

"Is it safe to stop in the towns?" Michael asked.

"Not entirely. But I'll go in on foot while you stay with the horses."

Archanus shook his head and the hint of a scowl crossed his handsome face

"If the Romans have begun looking for us this far from the scene of my crime," the Wise Man said, a note of sarcasm coloring his tone, "they'll be expecting two of us on horseback. A man alone won't be so noticeable."

The father and son ate in companionable silence. When they had finished, they covered their fire ring with sand from the creek side and cleaned up their campsite. Gathering their goods and strapping them to the backs of the horses, they planned their route of travel and discussed the destination they hoped to reach by evening.

"While we ride today," Michael said as they made their way down the hill, will you tell me again the stories of the Magi?"

"Of course." Archanus smiled, grateful that his son was interested in his heritage. "But you've heard these tales over and over. Don't you want to learn something new?"

"It might be a long time before you can tell me your stories again," Michael said sadly. "I don't want to forget anything about you . . . not anything at all."

His heart gripped by a sorrow too great to be borne, Archanus could not speak. Tears filled his chest and then his eyes as he hastened to take the lead so that his son would not witness his terrible grief.

CHAPTER
Four

The riders entered a long draw where the trail was narrow and the horses had to travel in single file. With Eleuzis taking his customary position in the lead, the little company proceeded in silence. The rugged terrain gave Archanus a chance to prepare for the tales he must tell. His own story was irreversibly intertwined with that of his wife so that now, one thread of history could hardly be unraveled without tugging at the cords of the other.

For a time, the Wise Man was held prisoner by the fear of pain that inevitably accompanies remembrance. When the path widened enough for the horses to walk side by side, he marshaled his courage and urged the somewhat lazy Spartan up alongside Michael and the fast-walking bay. As the horses matched strides, Archanus began to speak.

"My people are different from your mother's," he said, as if in mid-conversation. "It's not that either is better or worse than the other, just different." Archanus wavered, rethinking the statement. "No," he corrected himself, "that's not entirely true. In many ways, your mother's people are superior to mine. Somehow it seems that their understanding of the horses makes them better able to relate to humans."

"How can that be?" Michael wondered.

"The horsemen learn responsibility and caring and how to consider the needs of others above their own desires."

Archanus paused, recalling how Junia had found it so natural to think of him before she thought of herself. "Your mother's people value simple kindness," he finally went on. "They know how to love, and their faith is unquestioning. My own mother's people were like that. It is my father's sect, the Magi, that is complicated and always doubting, always searching for proof to substantiate their observations or assumptions."

"Tell me again why this sect is called the Magi," Michael encouraged. "I want to remember . . . "

"The Magi are an ancient order of priests." A sad smile softened Archanus' strong features. "Long ago, the Greeks thought us possessors of magical powers and gave us this name which, in their language, means magician, or sorcerer."

"But you're not sorcerers." As he spoke, Michael reached down unconsciously to stroke Eleuzis' fine neck.

Taking odd comfort in his son's natural love of the horses, Archanus laughed ironically. "Not the kind the name implies."

"What kind then?"

"Ours is a wisdom of the ages," said Archanus. "Throughout our history, we have studied the sun and the moon and the stars and observed how certain events in the heavens affect conditions on the earth."

"What sort of events?" Michael led his father on, knowing they were coming to a part of the tale he always enjoyed.

"We have seen how the tides in the great seas move in conjunction with the pull of the moon and how seasonal changes are heralded by the position of the sun on our horizon.

"We have watched what we first thought was the repositioning of the stars, and learned that this land we live on somehow shifts so that the sun and stars appear in different places during different seasons."

Archanus gazed off across the sweeping plain where the dry grasses heralded the end of summer. "We have observed that the moon seems to circle around us, while we apparently circle around the sun."

"I've never been able to understand what these things have to do with magic." Michael looked perplexed.

"That's because they have nothing to do with magic." Archanus squeezed Spartan's sides lightly, urging him to keep up with the long, easy striding Eleuzis.

"Our knowledge has done no more than to help us occasionally predict some earthly incident which we know will be brought about by activities we've perceived in the heavens. Because we've been able to make these predictions, we're called magicians."

"But you call yourselves scientists and scholars," Michael added, reining Eleuzis in, trying to stay beside his father.

"Yes, we're students of the universe," Archanus said.

"But most importantly, many of us wish only to be disciples of the One God. "

Suddenly, the conversation was interrupted when Spartan's hoof dislodged a rock and sent it tumbling down the hill that fell away from the path. At the unexpected noise, Eleuzis bolted sideways in a motion that would quickly have unseated a lesser horseman. Michael held his seat and instinctively reached down to calm the frightened horse, again stroking his neck and speaking softly. "All right." Michael's heart raced as he tried to calm his horse. "It's all right."

Reacting to Eleuzis' startled movement, Spartan stopped instantly, planting his feet with hard finality, raising his head, snorting, and flaring his nostrils to catch any scent of danger.

Under other circumstances, Archanus and his son might have taken lightly their horses' display of seemingly unwarranted fear. But not today. Alert for the trouble that stalked them, the man and the boy were anxious. The horses' distress turned to terror as they sensed their riders' unease.

Through the curious silent communication that passes between horse and horseman, the mildly frightening moment intensified rapidly into an incident of desperate horror, electrifying the very air. The tumbling of a rock loosened by a passing hoof took on the proportion of an enemy attack. Humans and horses incensed one another, fueling the fires of emotion, sending hearts racing, and accelerating the uncontrolled cycle of alarm and reaction.

The episode took place in little more than a minute. But the recognition of fear it fostered traveled with the riders far longer.

"I'm sorry, Son," Archanus said in the aftermath. "We can go on pretending that nothing is wrong, but we can't seem to fool these horses. They sense the tension we try to disguise, and they never stop watching for the danger we wish we could forget."

"Still," Michael said with the wisdom of one much older, "is it not better to pretend, than to let fear take us over?"

"Indeed it is." Archanus laughed, all but overcome by the pride he took in this rare and special boy.

In the wake of the incident, the father and son each retreated into his own thoughts. Their senses heightened to the extreme, they rode on in silence, neither able to escape the dread that held them in its lethal grip. Then, just as Archanus and Michael began to recover a degree of ease, the horses hesitated, raising their heads simultaneously, seeming to perceive yet another threat.

"Be still for a moment," Archanus said, reining Spartan to a halt.

Far ahead, a line of Roman soldiers, the sun glinting off their armor, traveled in single file. On a course perpendicular to that traveled by Michael and Archanus, the small cavalry unit would soon intersect this trail which the father and son must now abandon.

"Quick!" Archanus said, his voice filled with alarm. "We must hide ourselves. If we can see the soldiers, they can also see us."

"But where will we go?"

"Down into the ravine," Archanus spoke as he turned Spartan toward the incline that had become far more rugged as the path neared the crest of the hill.

"It's too steep here." Michael feared for the horses, though he worried little about his own safety.

"It's the only way!" Archanus exclaimed, urging Spartan over the precipice and down the steep incline.

In spite of his concern for the animals, Michael followed obediently, as his father knew he would. For moments that seemed like days, Eleuzis and Spartan plunged down the hill, their powerful haunches bunched beneath them, their manes flying, their forefeet barely glancing off the rough ground. As they crashed over the rocks and through the brush, Michael and Archanus could do no more than lean as far back as possible, giving the horses their heads so as not to obstruct their balance, praying silently, but passionately, that the One God would save them once again.

When at last they reached the bottom of the ravine, the riders struggled to regain their composure, stroking the necks of the horses whose sides heaved from the effort of their terrible descent. Fearful that the Roman brigade might have heard their noisy flight, Archanus cautioned Michael to remain quiet. Both horses stood remarkably still, their ears forward, alert for danger, though their heads hung low with exhaustion. Eventually, when no sound of approaching horsemen reached them, Archanus spoke. "We'll camp here tonight. There's plenty of water and the cover is good. Tomorrow we'll continue our journey."

The next day began much as every other. The only difference today was the heightened tension shared by the travelers following the preceding day's close encounter.

Each listening more carefully than ever for sounds that didn't belong to the morning, Archanus and Michael spoke little. Only after they had been riding for quite some time did they begin to relax and resume their conversation.

"Where were we yesterday?" Archanus asked as the pair rode beside the winding creek.

"You were telling me about the history of the Magi," Michael answered. "I've always wondered . . ." He paused. "Am I a Magi, or a horseman?"

"Both . . . actually . . . but by custom you are a Magi," Archanus said, a smile lighting his eyes. "You and I are direct descendants of the first high priest of the order."

"I want to hear the story again of where that first high priest came from."

"Tradition tells us that he was among those who escaped from Egypt with a Hebrew prophet called Moses. It is said that there was a time when the people who followed Moses out of Egypt became confused and began to worship golden idols instead of the One God. When that happened, Micah, who would one day be the first high priest of the Magi, set off on his own with a small company of followers, accepting his destiny as the father of our people."

"I was named for him, wasn't I," Michael said proudly.

"Yes," Archanus answered. "Do you remember what the name means in Hebrew?"

"Who is like Yahweh?" Once more Michael's tone held a note of pride. "And Yahweh is the Hebrew name for the One God."

"That's right . . . and Michael?"

"Michael means, Who is like God."

Up to this point, the ravine had provided natural cover. Now, as it opened out onto another vast plain, the companions faced the vulnerability of exposed travel. Sensing their riders' renewed tension, the horses proceeded in a halting, cautious gait, their heads high and ears forward, alert to impending danger. As the sun ascended toward its apex, the heat intensified and the riders fell silent.

"Is it good to be a Magi?" Michael asked later, renewing the conversation.

"Only if we use the gifts God has given us on His behalf," answered Archanus, glad for a break in the taut silence.

"If He gives us these gifts, doesn't He make us use them the right way?" Michael asked. "I mean wouldn't it be easier if He just told us what to do?"

"Perhaps." Archanus smiled. "But then we'd probably complain that He never let us make our own choices."

"So . . . will I be a Magi?" Michael persisted, turning in the saddle to face his father as Eleuzis' fast stride began again to distance him from Spartan.

"That's up to you." Archanus paused, choosing his next words carefully. "It is most important for you to know that you embody the best of all that your mother and I inherited from our ancestors and passed on to you.

You can be whatever you choose to be, follow any path you desire. You are not required to embrace the ways of the Magi or of the horsemen. We are not like many of the other peoples of this world who require that the sons follow in their father's footsteps. We hope . . . but we do not demand."

"And God? Will He at least help me to know what I should do?"

"If you continue to ask, and then listen for His answer, He will guide you," Archanus answered with a smile. "He doesn't want us to travel through this life without Him. He just doesn't force us to do anything. He has given us freedom of will . . . and that's a great responsibility."

"It's all kind of complicated, isn't it?"

"It seems to be. But I think it's just that we mortals insist on turning everything into a big mystery. The Hebrew people say that their God has simple plans for us all. They have ancient writings that seem to substantiate their claims."

"Who is their God?"

"He is the One God we seek. There are some people, like the Greeks, who believe that there are many gods. It is the Magi's belief that there is one, all powerful Creator. This Being is our One God."

"What does this God tell the Hebrews?"

"One of the things He says in those writings is: *Be still and know that I am God.*"

"What does He mean?"

"I think He is telling us to have faith in Him—to live our lives in peace and love and kindness, and to leave the rest to Him."

"But you can't be still, can you?" It was not exactly a question.

"No," Archanus said, "I can't seem to stop searching. I'm too curious. I want to know more. I want to understand the workings of our world and the skies above us. But more than anything, I want to come face to face with the One God who knows all things. Only then will my quest be over."

"Is that not where my mother has gone?" asked Michael, with obvious alarm.

"Yes, Son. She has gone to be with God in His heaven. But that's not where I am planning to meet Him just now." Archanus lightened the moment with a small laugh.

"I don't understand."

"According to Hebrew belief, the One God will soon send a Messiah to the earth to redeem His people. The Greeks call Him the Christ. I think the One God will be present when this Savior arrives."

"How will you know the time?"

"Long ago there was a Hebrew prophet by the name of Isaiah who foretold the coming of the Messiah. Isaiah described the Savior as the Son of God who would be a promise for the Hebrews and a light for the Gentiles."

"What is a Gentile?"

"Anyone who is not of the Hebrew faith . . . like us."

Where the trail fell into another long draw, Eleuzis again took the lead. Conversation ceased as the riders concentrated on the steep incline and the thriftiness of their horses' movements. At the foot of the hill they reached a sparkling stream.

"We'll stop here to rest the horses and let them drink their fill," Archanus said, as he rode up beside Michael.

While Eleuzis and Spartan grazed, the father and son shared a light meal, the last until they dared once again to enter a town for fresh provisions. Then they began their conversation again. "I still don't understand how you will know when the Christ comes," Michael said.

"Because of the Hebrew prophets' repeated references to light in relation to the Messiah, the Magi have always looked for signs in the heavens which might forecast His arrival. Our observations have led us to expect a great convergence of heavenly bodies which will cause a light brighter than any that has ever been recorded by our scientists. We believe this union of stars is the event planned by the One God to announce the birth of His Son and to lead us to the place of that blessed event."

"When will this happen?"

"We can only estimate," answered Archanus, "but we believe it will take place soon."

"Will you follow the star?"

"Yes," Archanus answered firmly.

"And will you be there for the Child's birth?"

"I hope to be, my Son. It is the sincerest of my desires."

CHAPTER
Five

They rode on in silence, each lost in his own thoughts and dreams. As the sun began its westward journey toward the night, Archanus and Michael lost sight, for a time, of their sorrows. They could not, however, disregard the terror that stalked them.

Soon it became obvious that the Wise Man could not go without sleep indefinitely. When they stopped for the night, Archanus asked his son to share the watch. It was a gesture that exhibited the Magi's growing respect for his son—an act that elevated the boy's confidence and deepened the relationship of the father and son.

As they traveled, a bond of friendship was forged between Archanus and Michael that would forever transcend the ordinary ties of blood. In the years ahead, each would call to mind this unique kinship of spirit and be drawn forward in their quest for reunion by the strength of its memory.

"Tell me again how you met my mother," Michael asked one day as the companions rode along. "I love that story."

"Were you reading my mind?" Archanus asked.

"I don't think so—"

"I was thinking about that encounter when you asked," Archanus explained. "It wasn't far from here that we were brought together for the first time. In fact, we should reach the place tomorrow."

"Are we nearing a town?" Michael asked with distaste.

"You are your mother's son." Archanus' blue eyes shown with fondness. "You dislike the confinement of civilization as much as she did."

"She taught me well," Michael said, looking off into the distance. "So, will you tell me again?"

"Yes, of course. I love the story too. It's a wonderful memory. Your mother's people and mine crossed paths in our travels. The Magi's study of the stars was leading us to the west, and the horsemen's journey toward summer grazing took them on a northeasterly course.

"One afternoon, my people were setting up camp on a hillside when the earth began to rumble. In the meadow below a great herd of horses galloped toward the stream that would be our source of water. Some among us were annoyed by the intrusion; but I, as always, was fascinated by the horses and the people who were their stewards."

The path narrowed and, as usual, Eleuzis took the lead. "Don't stop," Michael said, turning sideways on his horse to face his father. "I can hear you just fine, and Eleuzis doesn't need me to guide him."

"When our elders went to greet the leaders of the horsemen that evening," Archanus went on, "I tagged along. While the older men talked, I wandered out to the meadow to get a closer look at the horses.

"My father had told me that for generations these people had been considered the finest horsemen in all the world. It was said that these animals were descended from King Solomon's great herds and that they were so far superior to the horses of other tribes that there was no comparison. I wanted to see for myself."

"But you were a little afraid of the horses, weren't you?" Michael recalled.

"Oh yes." Archanus laughed. "I was no fool! I knew these could be fierce creatures, so I kept my distance. I was leaning against a rock, quietly enjoying the breathtaking power of the horses, when the most beautiful girl I had ever seen rode up beside me."

"Was she riding Eleuzis?"

"No. I don't think Eleuzis was even born at that time. If he was, he was just a colt. Anyway, that evening Junia sat astride a glorious black stallion that I could have sworn was snorting fire—"

A self-conscious smile lit the Wise Man's eyes at the memory of that encounter. "I stood my ground, though, pretending to be brave."

"She wasn't afraid of you, was she?" Michael helped his father along with the familiar tale.

"No. When she was with the horses, your mother feared nothing. At first she didn't trust me. She wanted to know what I was doing around her precious horses. I explained that I was awed by their strength and beauty. Once she was convinced that I meant them no harm, she condescended to talk to me. By the end of our conversation, I knew much more than I had before about the horses—and I was desperately in love with the girl who would one day become your mother."

"But that's not when you got married . . ."

"No." Archanus laughed again. "I probably would have married her then and there, but she was far too sensible and too involved with the horses. Besides, we were young. I was 15 and she was 13, not much older than you are right now."

They had reached the foot of another hill. Sunlight glanced off a thin stream of water that intersected their path, and the wary Eleuzis stopped hard before crossing. Planting his feet, lowering his head, and snorting, the big bay almost unseated his rider who still sat sideways, listening to his father's story.

"You silly beast." Michael laughed and patted Eleuzis' neck. "Isn't it funny," he said to Archanus, "how these horses will happily cross a big body of water but stop in panic when they come to a little stream like this."

"Your mother told me horses are apprehensive about creeks like this because they're so smart," Archanus said, patting Spartan's neck and urging him up beside Eleuzis. "She said they think these little streams are snakes, especially when they're sparkling in the sunshine."

Once the horses realized they had encountered water and not some fearsome creature, they dropped their heads and drank thirstily. When the animals finished drinking, the travelers resumed their journey. Spartan had to jog to keep up with Eleuzis' fast walk, but Archanus wanted to ride beside his son.

"After that first encounter," he began again, "we went our way, and your mother and her people went theirs. We didn't meet again until four years later. Ironically, it was at the same place. All those years I had dreamt of this girl. My parents were anxious for me to marry, but I could think of no one but the beautiful Junia. As it turned out, she was in the same predicament. We had fallen in love at our first meeting and neither of us would settle for anyone else."

"But you still didn't marry her."

"I wanted to. But she was still too sensible. She insisted we get to know one another first. Since she wasn't prepared to leave her beloved horses, I traveled with her people for some time before we were given to one another in marriage." A note of sadness had entered Archanus' voice as he talked, and for a little while he was lost in reverie.

"I'm sorry," Michael said. "I didn't mean to make you remember things that cause you sorrow."

"Don't be sorry. I'm only sad that I ever took her away from the horses. Until you were born, they were the greatest love of her life, and her last years were spent without them."

"She had the geldings," Michael reminded his father. "And surely she loved you most or she would not have left the horses for you."

"Perhaps," Archanus mused. "I always wondered though. And I always knew I was not being fair to her. She hated the cities where we had to live so that I could study and teach. She longed every day for the freedom of her nomadic people and for the horses that she viewed as the greatest symbol of that liberty."

"But she loved you," Michael said again. "When she talked to me of the things that were dearest to her, she always spoke of you first. Besides, she told me often that the One God called you to the city. She never thought you were being selfish."

"Then we are in the best of company." Archanus forced a smile. "Two men loved without reserve by an extraordinary woman. It is a gift not shared by many."

"She is with us, I think, even now," Michael said softly.

"Yes, Son, I believe you're right. I think she'll always watch over us in that special way she had of quietly caring. I know that we must be grateful for the time we had with her . . . " The Wise Man's throat closed over unshed tears.

"But it is much easier to be sad than thankful because we miss her so much." Michael finished the sentence for his father, and again the pair rode on in silence.

Since they came so close to encountering the Roman soldiers, Archanus and Michael had cautiously avoided both settlements and other travelers. For several days they had subsisted on water, roots, and the few berries that grew beside streams. For the horses, there was plenty of grass, so the animals kept their strength while the man and boy began to weaken.

The sounds of his empty stomach and the slight dizziness that had begun to overtake him frightened Michael. "We need something to eat," he said, breaking the long silence.

"I'm sorry, Son," Archanus said. "We can't take a chance on being recognized. Perhaps tonight we'll find something better to eat. And maybe soon we'll meet the horseman."

That afternoon the father and son arrived at the hillside where the Magi had set up camp so many years earlier when Archanus and Junia had first met. In the gathering dusk, almost as if the meeting had been planned, the horsemen came into the meadow below.

When the sun finished its descent behind the western horizon, the earth began to rumble. In the meadow below, a great herd of horses galloped toward the stream that had led Michael and his father to this place of rendezvous.

"Will we go to them tonight?" Michael asked, excitement and apprehension battling for priority in his young heart.

"Perhaps we should wait until morning." Archanus, too, was a victim of warring emotions. Michael's hunger was important. And yet, Archanus couldn't help but want to put off the inevitable encounter with Junia's brother, John.

It wasn't that he feared John's reaction to the news of his sister's death; he just wasn't looking forward to re-telling, and thereby re-living, the tale. "They'll be tired and they'll need to set up camp," he went on, trying to justify the delay. "It will be better if we wait."

There was no argument from Michael. Only the horses seemed anxious. Both geldings stomped impatiently and occasionally nickered at the grazing horses below. Finally, during the night, Michael got up and released Eleuzis and Spartan to rejoin the herd into which they had been born.

While Michael worried over the horses, Archanus was visited in his dreams by an angel of the Lord. "It is time that you let him go," the angel said. "He will be fine. From now on he will be protected by the Archangel whose name he bears."

"I cannot give him up," Archanus cried out in the dream. "He is the heart of my heart and the only light left in this dark night of my soul."

"Your night will pass," said the angel, "and for the child, the day is yet to begin. Each of you has a great commission, and you can only carry out your duties separately. As always, however, this is your choice. God will not force you. You must decide on your own."

"Will we see the coming of the Savior?" Archanus asked, a flicker of hope in his heart.

"I cannot answer that question," the angel said. "Only the One God knows what He has in store for you. I can tell you that He has plans to prosper you and not to harm you, plans to give you hope and a future. He loves you and your son, Archanus. He wishes to bestow upon you a great trust. It is for you to accept or to deny Him."

Archanus awoke with a start. Still feeling the presence

of the angel, he could not find enough logic to distort or to destroy the vision that still pulsed in his heart and his mind. The cool, gray light of morning had begun to illuminate the broad sky. Below, the great band of horses slaked the night's thirst in the stream that led them and their people through the valley between the mountains.

Archanus should not have been able to hear the rustling movements and snorts of the great creatures, nor should the conversations of the people who followed the herd have been so clear to him. But the angel had heightened the man's senses so he could listen to the sounds that would remind him of the life into which he would soon place his beloved son.

He could hear John, who had taken his father's place as the leader of the horsemen, telling his herdsmen that they would stay in this lush meadow and rest the animals for several days. There were women laughing and children scampering around an aromatic morning fire. The voices of the men were mellow as they ran gentle hands over the sleek and shining coats of their cherished horses. "These are good people," Archanus thought to himself, "and they are his family. He'll have a good life . . ."

"Still, how can I face the parting?" Archanus wondered as he watched his son who stood at the crest of the hill, looking down on the scene in the meadow. "How can I justify it to the boy? How can I live with the sorrow that will surely fill Michael's eyes at the prospect of yet another loss in so short a time?"

The Magi would obey his God, he knew that. He had planned to leave his son with his wife's people before the angel came to him, since this was, after all, the only safe course of action. Why, then, had this impending farewell suddenly become so difficult? Was it because the time had come, or because he felt some misplaced sense that the choice was no longer his own?

In his reasoning, scientific mind, Archanus arranged and rearranged, dissected and reassembled his thoughts until at last he could live with the decision which was, as the angel had said, his alone to make.

He would follow whatever course the One God charted for him. He would continue the quest on which he believed the One God had sent him. He might not feel the same joy he had once known at the prospect of this adventure. But he would obey. And he hoped that for his compliance he would one day be reunited with his son.

"It's time," Archanus said, walking up beside Michael. With a heavy heart, the Wise Man led the way down the mountain toward the horsemen, the parting, and an uncertain future.

CHAPTER
Six

The stream tumbled noisily toward the place where it fell over the edge of a great precipice into a sparkling pool. The horses, even more beautiful than Archanus remembered them, wandered at will through the camp, in perfect harmony with the humans who shared their tranquil existence.

A handsome bay stallion was the first to greet the father and son as they neared the camp. Michael reached a fearless hand toward the horse, and the powerful creature welcomed the boy, brushing his upturned palm with a muzzle as warm and tender as the kiss of an angel.

A woman waited at the edge of the clearing. Both she and her husband, Junia's brother, John, had been visited by an angel who told them their nephew and his father would soon arrive.

"Your sister's son will be left in your care," the angel had told them, "for the One God knows that you will raise him well and prepare him for the mission he has been chosen to accomplish."

"My name is Sarah. I am the wife of your mother's brother," the pretty woman said, reaching her hand out to Michael. "Come with me and we'll have some breakfast." Smiling, she led the boy away from his father and the men who had appeared beside him.

"We've been waiting for you," said a tall man with dark, merry eyes.

"It's good to see you," said another. "You must come and eat. Spend some time with us, before you continue your journey."

"You knew we were coming?" Archanus asked, only mildly surprised.

"We hoped so," said a third man. "From our Roman friend, Zadoc, we learned of your plight and prayed that you would come to us for help. We have chosen one of our finest horses to carry you as far as you need to go to find refuge."

Then John appeared. In the face of his wife's brother, Archanus could see the patience and the wisdom of the ages. In the moment when the two men's eyes met, the apprehension that had held Archanus in its deadly grip disappeared.

"We must talk awhile, my brother," John spoke gently, almost as though he were calming a fearful colt.

"Yes," Archanus said, relaxed by the kind tone of John's voice. "Yes, we need to talk."

The two walked away together and soon they found their way to the top of the hill where Archanus and his son had camped the night before. John was the first to speak after they had settled themselves on the crest where they could watch the herd below.

"The Roman soldiers came last week to pick out their new mounts," John said. "Our old friend, Zadoc, was with them."

"How many soldiers?" Archanus asked.

"Fifteen or twenty. Why?" John was puzzled.

"What day was it?"

"Midweek."

"So our fears were unnecessary." Archanus released a long sigh.

"Did you see the soldiers then?"

"Yes," Archanus said. "As we traveled up the long draw that climbs from the southern stream. Not far from the place where it intersects this path, we saw the soldiers and changed our course."

"You can't be sure it was Zadoc and his men," John offered.

"No, but the number of men and the timing is right." Archanus looked embarrassed. "When Zadoc left Michael and I, he said he was going to meet with the riders who were on their way to you. He cautioned us to take the long route to this valley so that we would come together with you after the Romans left . . . so, I should have known . . ."

"From what Zadoc told us, you have good reason to fear," John said. "And no reason to feel foolish for avoiding an encounter that might have meant your life!"

"Then you know the whole story," Archanus said, obviously relieved. "And that is why you expected us."

"Yes," John answered. "That's part of the reason . . . Sarah and I were also visited by an angel of the Lord who told us of your coming and offered us the opportunity to serve the One God by caring for Michael in your absence."

"But what do you know of Junia?" Archanus was grateful that John seemed glad to adopt Michael, but fearful that he would still be forced to relive the sorrow of losing his wife.

"We know that my sister perished when a strange malady took many in the town where you were teaching," John answered, laying Archanus' fears to rest. "And Zadoc has warned us that you are being hunted by the soldiers because the proconsul of the province has blamed you for this affliction."

"Tabeel, the proconsul, is a fool," Archanus said angrily. "His wife and son were among the first who became ill. In fact, I'm almost certain that they were the carriers of the disease."

"What makes you think that?" asked John.

"The physician in the town could not help the proconsul's wife and son, so the superstitious Tabeel, who believes that the Magi are sorcerers, decided to call on me."

"What did he expect of you?"

"A magical cure, I suppose," answered Archanus. "I tried to explain that I was a scientist and a teacher, not a healer, but he would have none of it. He left me alone with his wife, and she told me that they had just returned from a journey to Greece. Along the way, they encountered a band of nomads who were desperately ill. Against her husband's wishes she sent her handmaiden to the aid of a dying woman. That servant perished only days later, before they had returned to the city."

"The proconsul must have been aware of all this," John said. "Why then would he blame you?"

"It is not widely known that disease is transferred from one human to another," Archanus explained. "Most still believe that illness is a curse. Besides, Tabeel needed a scapegoat."

"And you were his choice."

"Indeed." Archanus shook his head sadly. "He was angry because I failed to do the magic he expected. And, since my own wife succumbed to the sickness almost at its outset, it was easy for Tabeel to convince the townspeople that I had brought the curse upon them. It didn't help that Michael and I did not become ill."

"How is that possible?"

"No one knows, really," Archanus said sadly. "Tabeel was not affected either. In fact, many men remained healthy although the women and children were stricken. I have seen similar plagues before, and it seems that the weaker, more exhausted a person is, the more dangerous the affliction. Women seem to be weakened by pregnancy . . ."

"I know that Junia carried another child," John said, placing a hand on Archanus' shoulder. "I'm sorry."

Archanus could not speak. Patiently, John sat beside his old friend. Finally he broke the silence. "So, the treacherous Tabeel was going to have you imprisoned?"

"Worse," Archanus answered, relieved at the change of subject. "If it hadn't been for Zadoc, Michael and I would not be alive today."

"Now you are a fugitive," John said, his voice heavy with sorrow. "Zadoc told us that he learned of the proconsul's plans and helped you to escape."

"At great danger to himself. He is a good friend."

"What now?"

"I fear that I will spend the rest of my life on the run. The Roman army is large, and all prevailing . . ." Archanus' voice trailed off.

"The Romans are so busy trying to conquer and control the world that they'll soon forget your minor infraction," John said firmly. "You won't be an outcast forever."

"Perhaps not," said Archanus. "But you agree that I must evade them until they have forgotten me?"

"I'm afraid so," John answered. "But you must stay a while and see your son has begun to adjust."

They had said what needed to be said, but neither man was ready to rejoin the others. In the hours that followed, Junia's husband and her brother shared their memories of the unique and beautiful woman they had each loved so well. By the time they returned to the horsemen's camp, Michael had already been given responsibilities and begun to establish the routine that would be his in the months and years ahead.

Archanus stayed for several days among the kindhearted horsemen, helping them break camp at the end of their interval in the meadow, traveling with them, wishing he could remain a part of their clan forever. But, of course, that wasn't possible. It was unthinkable to the Wise Man that his presence among them could cause horrible trouble for these good people.

On the morning of the seventh day in the company of his old friends, Archanus awoke with the clear understanding that this would be the day of their parting. He did not recall any angelic visit. He only felt a sure and certain knowledge that the time had come for him to depart.

As they stood among the others around the morning fire, warming themselves and preparing for the day, Archanus spoke to John. "I must bid you farewell," he said sadly.

"Yes," said John. "Go to Michael now. We understand that our good-byes need not be forever. The boy may not be able to see this so clearly."

"How can I leave him?" His assurance momentarily failing, the father's question was almost a sob.

"Only with the knowledge that he will be loved and protected by all of us. We are his family . . . and yours. One day you'll be able to rejoin us. Until then, I hope you can trust that we too are a part of the One God's plan and that we will obey just as you do."

"I cannot lie to you, John," Archanus said, looking off toward the north over the shining backs of the immense herd that spread like sand dunes in the sun across a vast expanse of open country. "At this point in my life, I have greater faith in you than I do in this God I've tried to follow. I can't help but feel He has forsaken me, and I do not know that I can bear His burden."

"Your faith will be restored," John said. "Come, you must take the boy aside now. God will give you the words to explain the necessity of your separation."

CHAPTER
Seven

They rode off together, the father and son; and for a time, the herdsmen wondered if either would return.

To carry Archanus on the continuation of his perilous journey, John had chosen a tall chestnut stallion, a horse of intrepid nature and great speed. The Magi would transport provisions in small packs behind his saddle. He could not afford to be slowed down by another animal laden with goods.

Michael rode beside his father on a lovely mare whose body coat matched that of the stallion but whose long mane and tail were the color of the sun. In the meadow below, Eleuzis and Spartan grazed peacefully, resting from the long and arduous trek they had just completed.

The *Lost Legend* • 83

"Where are we going?" Michael asked soon after their departure.

"To the top of that hill off to the east," Archanus answered. "There we can look upon this wide world and talk of things to come. "

"What is going to happen to us?"

"I wish I had an answer for that," Archanus said. "But I don't know. The One God has only made it clear to me that you and I have great commissions . . . and that we must fulfill them apart from one another."

"Must you leave us?" The boy knew the answer but didn't want to accept it.

"Yes, Son. You know it isn't safe for you or for the horsemen to have me in your company. But one day, my imagined crimes will be forgotten. You must believe, Michael. We *will* meet again—" His voice trailed off as the horses began their steep ascent.

The stallion surged ahead, taking the hill in great leaps, his powerful haunches and loins propelling him and his rider with fearsome speed up the steep incline. The mare, in spite of Michael's urging, chose a less rugged course, jogging easily along a switchback trail and arriving at the top of the hill not far behind Archanus and his horse.

The stallion's sides heaved. Foaming sweat escaped from beneath his saddle and all along the wide line where the reins rubbed against his neck. The mare, showing no signs of exhaustion, shook herself lightly and dropped her lovely head to savor the sweet grass of the clearing on which they stood.

"Let's sit awhile," said Archanus, stepping down from his horse, taking the reins over the animal's head, and trying to encourage him to enjoy the sweet grass as did

Michael's mare. But the stallion stood proudly, his head high, a sentinel, alert and prepared for flight.

Michael took the bridle off of his mare and laid it in the grass. Then he sat down beside his father and waited.

"I don't know where to begin," Archanus said with uncharacteristic confusion. "I'm not certain what I am to do or where I am to go." He paused and bowed his head for just a moment as if in prayer. It seemed a long while before Archanus spoke again. When he did, his voice held new hope and fresh resolve.

"You have been chosen by the One God for great honor. You will live with your mother's family for a time, and then you will begin your own assignment. I have not been given the details of your mission or my own. I have only been assured that when the time comes, each of us will be ready."

Archanus paused and looked at his son for a long moment as if trying to memorize every line and angle of the boy's beautiful face.

"Your time with the horseman will prepare you," he went on at last. "They'll teach you the skills you'll need. Your mother's family has abilities I do not share. You will become adept at these things so that you can carry out that for which you have been chosen—"

Archanus' voice seemed to dissolve, caught by the gentle breeze that wafted across the hillside. Again the companions lapsed into silence.

Finally, Michael spoke. "Why must you go? Why can't you stay with me while I learn and travel with me on this mission of mine?"

His words trembled with emotion. "Why did my mother have to die? Why does my father have to leave me?" Now his own voice trailed off in a sob.

Archanus put a strong arm around his son but for a while said nothing. The wind began to pick up. The chestnut stallion stomped impatiently. The mare continued to graze, content to await the will of her boy.

"I have asked the same questions," Archanus said at last. "I don't understand God's timing, but I know this is all a part of His plan. And, I have begun to take some comfort in a bit of wisdom given me by our friend, Zadoc. He said perhaps the One God loved your mother too much to leave her in this dreadful land any longer, so He took her home to be with Him, to live forever in peace and safety."

"Does He not love us?"

"Oh yes!" Archanus smiled for the first time since the conversation began. "Yes, He loves us . . . enough to let us serve Him as no other will have the opportunity to do."

"But why must we do these things alone?" Michael persisted, still not ready to accept the forced separation.

"Because I am a fugitive . . . and because our tasks take place in different parts of the world," Archanus said, becoming aware of this latter reality only as he spoke it. "We must complete the missions entrusted to us in the One God's time. I must travel one direction, you another. There is not enough time for us to go together to both places and to accomplish all that we must in each."

His father's mysterious knowledge did not seem strange to Michael. Having been raised in the company of a man whose apparent communication with the One God was as natural as his interaction with the humans around him, Michael accepted readily all that his father said, though his belief did not allay his distress.

"When will we meet again?"

"I can't answer that, Son," Archanus said, looking deeply into the eyes of the boy who would, he thought, too soon be a man. "It is promised that we will be reunited. We must hold on to this knowledge, and to our love for God and each other. No matter what happens in the years ahead, no matter how long it takes, we must chart our varied courses by the Star of Faith that will one day guide us back to one another. We cannot succumb to fear or disillusionment. We must believe."

Once more, silence fell like a veil, as the father and son gazed together toward some unknowable point on the distant horizon. Their hearts beating in unison, their thoughts traveling parallel paths, the wayfarers were given the strength by the One God they served to say farewell and to carry on. After a lengthy interval, Archanus and Michael rose and stood side by side, symbolically facing their uncertain futures.

Around Archanus' neck hung two leather thongs from which were suspended a pair of amulets. The jagged edges of the icons, when placed side by side, fit perfectly together. On one side of each were printed the letters *Miz*, on the reverse sides, the letters *pah*.

Archanus reached up and took one of the cords from his neck, then moved to place it around the neck of his son.

"Wait," Michael said, reaching out to look at the talisman. "This was my mother's. You must keep it. It will protect you." The boy's voice was fearful. "Nothing can happen to you," he hurried on. "My mother will keep you safe."

"And what of you, my son?" Archanus smiled.

"The One God will watch over me," Michael answered with assurance. "You have told me so."

"Just as He will protect me," Archanus said patiently. "These trinkets are not gods . . . and they cannot offer us protection. Only the One God has that power. These pieces of stone are simply reminders of our love for one another and of the promise God has made to bring us back together."

Michael inclined his head slightly as Archanus slipped the cord around his son's neck. Only then did Michael recall what the words meant. "My mother used to raise this medal to her lips and kiss it. One day I asked her what it said."

"What did she tell you?"

"May the Lord watch between me and thee." Michael looked into his father's eyes, reciting the prayer that now hung round each of their necks.

"When we are absent one from the other," Archanus and Michael said in unison.

Following another lengthy silence, the father and son began to make ready for their departures. "I will not bid you good bye," Archanus said, enfolding Michael in his strong arms. "Until we meet again —" He could not go on.

"I will live for that day." Michael spoke into his father's chest, a note of defiance in his tone. "I will obey. I will learn. I will complete my mission. But my heart will seek you always, and I will not rest until the day of our reunion."

There was nothing more to say. Archanus released Michael from his powerful embrace and looked longingly into the boy's eyes. As he climbed into the saddle, he said, "Look for me when you see the Star that heralds the birth of the Savior." And then he rode away.

Michael remained atop the hill watching as his father rode north and east, away from the setting sun. Only when he could no longer see the horse and rider, did the boy leave his post and begin his descent into the valley below.

CHAPTER
Eight

For many days following his father's departure, Michael's heart ached with such ferocity that he could not be consoled. Sarah and John's kindness served only to intensify his pain. Soon he began to avoid human contact, spending more and more time alone with the horses.

Helpless in the face of their nephew's sorrow, John and Sarah looked for ways to keep Michael busy. They hoped that if his mind were occupied, he would have less time to think of the pain in his heart. Gradually they increased the boy's responsibilities for the care of the herd, and before long, he was the favored assistant of his mother's cousin, Zimri, the healer.

Each morning, Michael rose ahead of the sun to begin his routine. He took it upon himself to inspect the entire herd, making certain every mare, and foal, and stallion was healthy and without injury. He became Zimri's sentinel, the only individual upon whom the healer had ever depended so completely.

In the beginning, when his morning chores were completed, Michael would ride off alone on Eleuzis. Sometimes he would scout the trail ahead. Other times he would ride the perimeter of the herd observing the ways of the animals, coming to know each one personally. The inseparable companions could often be seen loping easily across a broad meadow with Eleuzis' black mane flying in the wind, brushing the face of the boy who sat so easily astride the great, bare back of the big horse. From a distance they appeared as one, with no separation between bodies, perhaps even without delineation of spirit or soul.

Michael was an agile, athletic youngster who craved both physical and mental challenge. Although Eleuzis was not a young horse, Michael began teaching the animal to do small tricks like laying down and allowing the rider to climb on his back, bowing, or standing on his hind legs for long moments. To test himself further, Michael learned to stand on the horse's back. Beginning this self-test while Eleuzis stood grazing, the youthful horseman soon mastered the art of standing aboard his horse's back in perfect balance at the walk, the trot, and the gallop.

One afternoon when Michael, now fourteen years old, had been with the horseman for two years, John looked up to see the boy standing on the back of Eleuzis at a full gallop. With the great strides that belonged only to horses of his height and flexibility, Eleuzis seemed to devour the uneven ground in a wide open race with the wind. Michael's arms, outstretched in a posture of reverence and utter abandon, could have been the wings by which this exuberant pair flew. The boy's head was thrown back, a smile filled his eyes and shaped his young mouth. His countenance was suffused with the light of pure, unfettered joy.

Confusion overtook John as he watched. He could not help but be thrilled by the spectacle. Yet, the absolute lack of fear in his young charge filled the man's heart with foreboding. What if the horse stumbled? Or spooked? What if the boy lost his balance and fell beneath the feet of the charging animal? All at once, John had the awful feeling that Michael was slipping away.

"Quite a sight, isn't it?" Sarah had walked up beside her husband while he was lost in thought.

"Why hasn't it been obvious before?" John spoke as if she could read his thoughts. "It's so evident now."

"You mean that Michael is losing contact with people?" Sarah said, confirming John's assumption that she could read his thoughts.

"Yes," John said, shaking his head sadly. "Even as this fine young horseman is developing a powerful bond with the horses, he's disconnecting from his people. How could I not have seen the way he talks to the horses as though they can fully understand him?"

"We have all watched and done nothing," Sarah said. "For some time I've noticed that he rarely speaks except to converse with Zimri over matters relating to the animals."

"He has no trust in us." John's voice was filled with guilt and sorrow.

"How can he trust us when in his heart he feels abandoned by the two people a child must be able to trust beyond all others?" Sarah said.

"But they didn't abandon him."

"His mind may know this. But his heart does not." Sarah placed a loving hand on her husband's arm.

"I'm afraid he's even lost sight of the One God," John said. "His only faith seems to be in the horses."

"For now, his broken heart can only be touched by the animals," Sarah said softly.

"Perhaps we haven't tried hard enough to reach him."

"He's needed time to heal on his own." Sarah placed a tender hand on her husband's cheek, turned him toward her, and looked into his eyes. "We have not failed your sister's son," she said, understanding the root of John's concerns. "We have stayed out of his way so that he could grow freely and master the lessons the One God sent him here to learn. Perhaps it is time now for us to begin teaching him those things he hasn't yet found."

"Such as?"

"The faith of his father and mother," Sarah began. "Training the horses for work, not only for his own pleasure . . ."

"That's it!" John said excitedly. "He can work with Jephthah. He can learn to start the colts and to finish the training of the older horses. He'll be the best there ever was at this . . ."

"And it will offer him the challenge he seeks," Sarah said wisely. "He'll also have to talk with and listen to another person. But, will Jephthah be willing?"

"Yes, I believe he will." John smiled. "They're much alike, those two. Both communicate with the horses far more readily than they do with people. Besides, I've seen

Jephthah watching Michael with interest and admiration. I think he'll be glad to have the chance to work with the boy."

John's prediction was correct. Jephthah welcomed the opportunity to work with Michael, and the pair became fast friends. Each was gifted of God with innate understanding of the horses, and they related to one another as naturally as they related to the horses. It was through his friendship with Jephthah that Michael began to trust humankind once again.

Little by little, with the same patience that made him a fine horseman, the older man taught his young pupil to let down his guard. Surprisingly, since he wasn't known to be a man of great faith, it was also Jephthah who gently led Michael into the journey toward the One God by whom the boy had too long felt utterly abandoned.

One day, as they were riding through the herd giving names to the young horses they would soon begin to train, Michael asked, "Where did your name come from, Jephthah?"

"My mother's mother was a Hebrew. Mine is the name of one of my grandmother's ancestors."

"What does it mean?"

"Yahweh frees." Jephthah smiled.

"Yahweh . . . the One God," Michael murmured. "Do you believe the One God set you free?"

"Yes, I do. Each of us who seeks freedom finds it in a different way. Mine came through the horses."

"Were you not born a horseman?"

"No. I was saved by these good people from a life of slavery and degradation. I wasn't much older than you are when they rescued me."

"How did this happen?"

"My people were shepherds. We were attacked by desert pirates while moving our sheep to summer pastures. My parents were killed. My sisters and I were captured. We were being taken to Persia to be sold into slavery when we encountered the horsemen. Our captors decided to steal new mounts, but they weren't prepared for the courage and strength of these people."

"What happened?"

"Those evil men did not live to take another life."

"And what of your sisters?"

"They too became members of this family. You've seen them often. The oldest is the wife of Zimri, the healer."

"Do you still grieve for your parents?" Michael asked, wondering if his friend shared the awful sadness from which he could not seem to free himself.

"I miss them deeply," Jephthah answered. "But I have come to understand that God finds a way to bless us, even in the face of terrible tragedy. He always offers some gift, some consolation. For me, His gift was the horse. To ease my grieving, He gave me the great gift of freedom that these noble creatures represent to all who come to know them. Once I recognized this, I began to thank Him. The horsemen saved me from unspeakable horrors. And the horses have provided me with the greatest physical liberty a man can hope to know."

"Did the horses also free your spirit?"

"Only through the One God can we have true freedom of spirit. He has given us the horses to show us the way on our journey toward Him. He knows our hearts, and He releases us from every heart-held burden. We have only to allow Him to do so."

For a time, the companions lapsed into silence. Then, concerned that Michael was dwelling too deeply on his own sorrows, Jepthah asked, "What of your own name?"

"I too am named for an ancestor—the first high priest of the Magi," Michael said, sounding relieved to have been drawn from his reverie.

"Did your father also tell you that Michael is one of the greatest of the angels?"

"He did!" the boy explained, all at once remembering something he had not thought of for too long. "My father said that Michael is an Archangel and that I am greatly blessed because this angel is my protector."

"You are, indeed, uniquely blessed. The Hebrews believe that the Archangel Michael is the One God's fiercest warrior."

"How do you know so much?"

"My mother was very proud of her heritage. She

taught me the language and many things about the history of her people."

"Will you tell me the things she taught you?"

"It is good for me to have such a willing student," Jephthah said. "In time I'll share all that I know with you."

"You have made great progress with Michael," John said to Jephthah one evening as the two men sat beside the campfire.

"How do you see this progress?" Jephthah asked.

"You have touched his carefully guarded heart and helped him to overcome his fear of the people who love him. How have you managed this?"

"A boy and a horse are not so different from one another," Jephthah said, smiling. "With each, the teacher must be patient, gentle, and persistent. Both must be coaxed and drawn toward that which they will soon consider natural and comfortable."

"Why do you suppose you were able to reach Michael when Zimri could not?" John asked.

"Zimri is accustomed to healing physical illness and injury. I am in the habit of dealing with the heart and the spirit. Michael was not physically disabled. Only his heart and his spirit were wounded."

"And now he is well?"

"Not entirely." Jephthah spoke with caution. "A boy so young should not have to face such loss. He will never be like the other boys. He will always be old and wise beyond his years, more serious than most. He'll be one who passes through childhood without recognizing its pleasures on his way to becoming a great man."

"But he does play, now and then," John said, feeling sad and somehow guilty for all that he knew his nephew was missing.

"Yes, he plays," Jephthah said. "With the horses. But have you ever seen him running and testing himself with the other boys?"

"No." There was deep sadness in John's eyes. "No, I've never seen that. He doesn't even talk with them."

"They're too young for him," Jephthah said. "He doesn't relate to them at all. Michael is a man in a boy's body. We must teach him what we can, and then we must let him go. It won't be long before he will leave us to undertake the mission for which the One God has chosen him."

CHAPTER
Nine

Time passed. Michael continued to work with and learn from both Zimri and Jephthah. The days stretched into months and the months into years. The beautiful boy grew into a handsome young man, a horseman of unparalleled skill and compassion. Although a person of increasing knowledge, Michael still struggled with his faith.

In their vast wanderings, the horsemen came regularly into contact with people of various cultures. Before Michael joined the family, these encounters were, for the most part, purely social. But this son of a Magi carried within him the fine mind and curiosity of his father, and from everyone he met, he learned. His remarkable gift of listening and his unequaled memory helped the boy to become a storehouse of all manner of information until, at a very young age, his wisdom approached that of his exceptional father.

The Lost Legend • 105

Always seeking word of his father, Michael would sit late into the night listening to the conversations of the men who shared tales of the road and argued about the politics and religions of the day. He rarely spoke to anyone other than his teachers, his aunt, and his uncle. He never interrupted his elders during these fireside sessions. In his quiet, intelligent way, he simply absorbed and stored for future reference the information that was casually bandied about. Even more attentive than usual on those rare occasions when his people came in contact with members of the Magi, he refused to give up the hope that, one day, he would encounter someone who had word of Archanus.

It was during one such rendezvous with five traveling Magi that Michael heard again the prophecy of the Star that would rise above the birthplace of a King.

"The Star will lead us to our Savior," said the Magi known as Balthazar. "A Child will be born to free the world from the bondage of greed and cruelty that are the real earthly rulers in this tyrannous Roman Empire."

How desperately Michael wanted to jump up and shout, "My father knew that! Before he went away, he told me this Child was coming. He said to watch for him at the coming of this Star. We must find him so that he can be there."

But he didn't speak. His habit of silence was too deeply ingrained.

John caught a glimpse of the intent look in the boy's eyes. "Come, my son," John said. "Join us. You are old enough to take part in these discussions."

Michael nodded, solemnly stepping forward and taking a seat between John and Balthazar. "Thank you," he said, turning his attention once again to the Magi.

For a long moment, Balthazar gazed silently at the handsome youth who had just stepped from the shadows to join the gathering. There was something familiar about this young man. Something he couldn't quite place. Unable to pinpoint or to shake the feeling, he pushed it aside. Deciding he must be mistaken, the Magi leader began to speak again.

"The Savior will lead the world with a scepter made of love. He'll be a soldier whose sword and shield are fashioned of faith in His Father, the One God." Balthazar paused, taking time to look individually into the eyes of each one present. "The world will never be the same once He has come," the Wise Man continued at last. "The most respected members of our sect will follow the Star to the birthplace of the Son of the One God, and they will present our gifts to this Child who will be known as the Prince of Peace."

"Who will be chosen from among you?" John asked.

"We do not know," replied Balthazar. "There was once a man whose exalted stature in our ranks guaranteed his place as the leader of that expedition. His name was Archanus, and he was a direct descendant of our first high priest, Micah. We met on only two occasions so I did not know him well, but his wisdom was legendary."

"What has happened to this Archanus?" John asked, fearing the answer, but also wanting to allay any suspicions the Magi might have about Michael. As the boy matured and the angles of his face strengthened, he looked more and more like his father. Soon all that would be left of Junia were the striking blue eyes.

Balthazar's obvious puzzlement as he studied Michael emphasized the possibility that the boy could be recognized. John would never forget Zadoc's warning of treachery within the Magi. Balthazar was an old and trusted friend—but what of his companions? For this boy, whom he had come to love as his own, the horseman would give his life. So it was simple to skirt the truth for diversion, and, if the news was bad, he would find a way to deal with the consequences.

"Sadly," Balthazar answered, "Archanus has been lost to us. A wicked Roman proconsul accused him of cursing a whole city with an illness that killed many. Following the death of his own wife, our brother was forced to flee, and now he has disappeared. We seek him still, but we fear the worst."

The rushing of his blood roared in Michael's ears. He felt certain that all those gathered must be aware of the hot flush on his cheeks and the violent beating of his young heart. Still he did not speak. He had been taught well that he must not reveal his true identity, a secret held safe by his mother's family who took seriously their responsibility to protect him. No matter how trustworthy anyone might appear, the horsemen kept their own counsel, never revealing the truth about Michael.

Night and day after that meeting, Michael's great mind was consumed by thoughts of the coming King, hoping that his father would find a way to attend the heralded Birth. One day, several months later, John returned from a scouting expedition looking tired, but excited.

"I have news of your father," John said, almost breathless as he rode up beside Michael. "The Magi believe that Archanus is alive. He was seen in the country north of the Great Sea. It is said that he is a teacher in this land, that he is traveling from town to town under a new identity."

Aware that Michael desperately wanted to interrupt, John hurried on. "Wait, I'll answer your questions soon, but there is more. I was told that the time is near and that three of the most honored of the Magi have been chosen to take treasures to the birthplace of the Savior . . . and among those is our friend, Balthazar."

"What about my father?" Michael asked his eyes alight with mingled fear and longing. "Will he join the party that follows the Star?"

"As Balthazar told us when he last visited our camp, your father would have led the expedition had he been able to come out of hiding. In his absence, Balthazar and two others of the sect were chosen to follow the Star."

Michael felt the helpless sting of injustice and the prickle of unwanted tears behind his eyes. "It should have been my father," he said sadly. "He wanted it so . . ." Though the spiritual battle in his heart raged on, it had become less common for Michael to question the One God's wisdom. This news, however, brought back all of his old doubts, laid open all the wounds of his losses. "I need to go tend to the young stock," he said after a long silence. And John could do nothing but watch him go.

In the ensuing months Michael was torn by conflicting emotions. On the one hand he was deeply grateful for the news that his father was alive. On the other he felt mingled sorrow and outrage that Archanus would not be among the Magi who would pay homage to the Baby King.

John and Sarah watched sadly as the terrible anguish played itself out in Michael's young heart. "How desperate the spirit of the one who has no recourse against that which he perceives as unjust," John said to his wife one night as they lay near the fire talking of their nephew.

"How will Michael fare in this awful battle?" Sarah whispered. "He so passionately wishes to convince the One God that His course of action is wrong. I fear the boy will be consumed by his feelings of injustice."

"The good heart cannot sustain such conflict for long," John said. "And Michael's heart is truly good. He will come around."

John was right. In time, Michael succumbed to a kind of uneasy truce with this God whom he still thought he would never understand. It wasn't until the boy gave up the inner struggle that his own role in the drama ahead began to unfold.

On a night that was strangely dark, Michael lay sleeping uneasily. Dense clouds hung heavy beneath a moonless sky, obscuring the stars and turning eerie the gentle sounds of the pulsing darkness. A mare and her colt stood nearby, asleep but alert, facing away from the light breeze that led the clouds across the resting land. Deep into the second watch of that starless night the angel who had come to Archanus years earlier returned with a message for Michael.

"Your time has come," the angel declared. "In the morning you will begin your journey."

"But where must I go?" Michael asked. "And how will I travel?"

"I cannot reveal your destination, but you will be guided every step of the way," the angel told him. "You will know the horses you are to choose for the journey. They will carry you with strength and courage. Your people will send you away with their blessings. In your travels you will be protected by the angels who will come in response to the prayers of those who love you."

"If this is the mission my father and my teachers have spoken of, I am still afraid," Michael said with typical openness. "I fear I am not yet ready. Perhaps I never shall be —"

"You have learned your lessons well and faithfully," the angel assured him. "Now you will use the knowledge and the wisdom you have gained to serve the One God your father still diligently seeks."

"Then my father is alive," Michael whispered. "He really is alive?"

"Yes," said the angel, "and his prayers are always with you. He has made peace with our God, and his faith will be rewarded."

"Will I see him, then? Will he be there? Will we join Balthazar and the others at the birth of the Child?" Michael's questions came in an unrestrained rush.

"I cannot answer these questions," the angel said. "You will know in God's own time. As your father had to do when he left you with your mother's people, you must now choose. It is yours to decide whether or not to obey God's wishes."

"But I must have angered this God. I have fought with Him, questioned Him. How can He forgive me?"

"Do not confuse the Almighty God with yourself," the

angel replied. "You are weak, but He is strong . . . and He loves you without condition."

"Still," Michael said dispiritedly, "I am only a boy. How can I be of any use to Him? How can I set off alone and do Him honor?"

"Fear not," the angel said. "God Himself goes before you. He will never leave you nor forsake you. Do not be afraid or discouraged. You have been chosen above all others to bestow a priceless gift upon the Son of God, and upon the world that will one day be His."

"Then it is the Baby King I go to meet," Michael said, his voice trembling with the enormity of his impending mission.

"It is," said the angel. "But I can tell you no more. You must have faith. Only this will save you from the dangers that lie ahead. Do not doubt," the angel finished. And then he was gone.

CHAPTER
Ten

In the morning, the little camp bustled with activity. The women prepared large quantities of food while the men filled many goatskins with water and gathered supplies for a long, solitary journey. Michael wondered how they knew it was time for him to leave, but he did not ask. Instead, he quietly began to make his way through the herd of horses he dearly loved.

Over the years, it had become plain to Michael that all of the stories his mother and father told him about these horses were true, if slightly understated. These were, indeed, the heartiest and most beautiful animals of their kind in all the known world. Descendants of those sturdy creatures that had apparently originated in the desert between Persia and Palestine, this herd represented the best of the best. Culled and nurtured by the finest horsemen of the day, these were the animals most highly sought after, not only by the soldiers, but by royalty throughout the Roman Empire. Now, the time had come for Michael to choose the sturdiest and most stalwart of this exceptional band.

As he passed through the sea of fine horseflesh, he murmured endearments to those he knew he would not soon see again. Touching a flank here, a shining mane there, he made his way from one end of the herd to the other. It wasn't until he was halfway through his inspection that he realized he was being closely followed by the little mare that had owned his heart since the day of his father's departure when he rode her to the top of the hill to bid Archanus farewell. A chestnut beauty with the most exotic head and the largest, blackest eyes in the herd, she was called Lalaynia. It was Michael and his Aunt Sarah's great sorrow that the ten-year-old Lalaynia, though she had been many times with a stallion, had failed to bear a foal during the three seasons that preceded this fateful morning.

"No, my sweet girl," Michael said, running his hand along the mare's neck to her withers. "You can't go with me. You're too dear, too small, too beautiful . . . and I love you much too much."

The mare looked at her boy with understanding eyes and simply continued to follow him. When he had inspected and seriously considered every possibility and was still unable to make a decision, Michael turned to Lalaynia. As though she could answer, he asked, "What shall I do, girl? Which of your friends do I choose to carry me on this mission?"

Still the mare gazed patiently at her human, waiting, it appeared, for the boy to come to his senses and recognize what she knew instinctively. In the end, it was Sarah who helped Michael to understand what his decision must be.

"Lalaynia is not old enough to be barren," the woman said. "She will have to be sold off and she could be ill-used, or worse. She is God's choice for you. She will serve Him, and you, better than any other animal could."

"But she's so small," Michael said. "How will I carry provisions?"

"You'll take another horse." Sarah laughed. "Let the mare choose her companion—the animal that will carry your supplies. It is the God of your father who has given me these words. You must have faith, Michael. Do not question; just believe."

"Why in the world would He choose a lowly horseman and a little, barren mare for a mission of any importance?" Michael asked.

"That's how the One God works." Sarah smiled patiently, brushing a heavy lock of hair out of Michael's eyes. "He doesn't choose the rich or powerful to do His bidding. He looks for those who will rely on Him because they do not consider themselves invincible." Sarah paused for a long moment and looked deeply into Michael's still questioning eyes. "You must remember this and never become too self-important. Only with the help of God can you triumph in this life.

"Pay attention to Lalaynia," Sarah added, turning to walk away. "She'll always help you to make the right choices."

Michael watched as the woman who had become his mother walked away. Believing in Sarah's wisdom, he led Lalaynia back into the herd to choose the animal that would share their travels. Much to Michael's dismay, Lalaynia walked over to an aging black gelding and rested her muzzle on his withers. A horse that had aided well his masters for too many summers, Ghadar was the last animal Michael would have chosen to carry his goods on this mission.

"No." Michael laughed. "Ghadar is too old to go with us. We need a young horse with great strength and endurance." His voice caught on a silent sob as he thought of Eleuzis, the wonderful horse that had served him, and his mother before him, so well for so long. He considered Eleuzis the last link with his mother, and sometimes he missed the horse desperately. Two summers earlier, Eleuzis' great heart had ceased its rhythmic beating. Michael wondered, as he had so often, if the big bay was now carrying Junia over the hills and through the canyons of heaven.

"Ghadar is Lalaynia's brother." John, who had walked up behind Michael, spoke softly, interrupting the boy's sad thoughts. "He has been one of the strongest and most fearless of all the horses I have ever known."

"He has been," Michael said. "But now he is old and deserves a good life, grazing these fields . . . not a perilous journey from which he may not return."

"You fear for yourself," John said, "not Ghadar."

"I am only cautious."

"And so is he," John said gently. "God has chosen this brave horse who will serve you as he has served us all these many years. His wisdom, his sensibility, will save you where a younger horse's skitishness would place you in grave danger. Have faith, Michael. Do not doubt."

When it came time for the little company to depart, all of the horsemen and their families gathered together to say a fond and loving farewell.

"Our hearts and our prayers go with you," John said, his voice now husky with emotion.

"This will not be our last good-bye," Sarah said, hugging the tall man-child, resting her tear-stained face on his broad, young chest.

"We will join you, somewhere down this road we all travel," said another.

Michael could not speak. His heart was too heavy at yet another parting. He tried to check the tears that welled-up in his eyes, but finally let them flow without shame. Then all at once, he summoned that spark of courage that had long sustained him. The same passion that had kept him from giving in to a sorrow beyond bearing, would strengthen him for the dangerous journey he must now undertake.

"You are my family," he said at last. "I will find my father and we will return. I know not when or how, but we will rejoin you."

With that, he swung gracefully up onto the back of the lovely Lalaynia and with her brother, Ghadar, they headed across the valley toward a thousand tomorrows.

So it was that a boy of just sixteen years set off aboard an apparently barren mare with an aged gelding carrying the goods that would nourish the little trio on this most important pilgrimage. It did not seem odd to Michael to allow Lalaynia to chart the course. Once he had accepted the choice of these horses, which had obviously been made for him, it was easy to place his trust in them.

Michael's inner conflict with the One God, however, remained unresolved. He wanted to feel the Divine confidence expressed by his parents. But he could not. Belief in tangibles—things and people and events he could see—was easy. Trusting in a mysterious God whom he could neither see, nor feel, was another matter.

Intellectually, this brilliant young man could accept the idea that there was a God directing the good people and the angels he had encountered in his brief life. But there were terrible roadblocks between his head and his heart. The greatest of these obstacles was Michael's inability to understand how a Being as loving and omnipotent as this God was reported to be could allow such pain and suffering to go on in the world.

"Perhaps," he whispered to his horses as they set out, "I will find the answers on this journey."

CHAPTER
Eleven

For endless days the comrades traveled alone on a heading west by northwest, out of the Persian mountains to the plain where the Euphrates wound its way toward the Mediterranean Sea. With his mother's people, Michael had traveled this route before, so all but the aloneness was familiar.

The horsemen had sent Michael on this expedition with all that they could gather in the way of trinkets and treasures to trade for supplies, and he found no difficulty procuring everything he needed along the way.

It had always been necessary for anyone traversing this land to avoid, and when avoidance failed, to do battle with the pirates of the desert who systematically plundered travelers. But mysteriously, as this trek began, Michael saw no highwaymen, was accosted by no one. When this occurred to the boy, he realized that, once again, he and his horses were surrounded by an army of invisible angels, just as he and his father had been shielded long ago. For many days and nights, these angelic guardians warded off all peril . . . until that fateful evening a fortnight into the journey when the attack came.

Lalaynia was making her careful way along a narrow trail which wound dangerously into a steep ravine. By today's measurements, their destination lay at least half a mile away following the switchback path—or some 150 feet straight down.

It was the time of the long shadow, when the day receded toward the night. For days, Michael had heard no sound save the rhythmic clip, clop of Lalaynia's and Ghadar's hooves, when all at once a band of shabbily clad riders rushed at the boy and his horses. Appearing, it seemed, from nowhere, they whooped and shouted loudly, mindless of the treacherous ground beneath the feet of their scraggly mounts.

It was the first occasion when Michael fully realized the wisdom of John's statement that he would be grateful for Ghadar's good sense. When a younger, less seasoned horse might have bolted in fear of the flashing swords and the wild shouts of the drunken band, Ghadar held his position, stolid and forbearing. Lalaynia, too, remained quiet, and the calm of his companions saved Michael from a panic that might otherwise have overtaken him.

"How do we fight back?" Michael uttered aloud. "I have no weapon, and we are grossly outnumbered."

Shouting and gesturing wildly, the savage pirate horde seemed to be everywhere at once.

Suddenly, the leader was upon Michael and Lalaynia. Grabbing the mare's bridle, the ugly assailant tried to force the horse and her boy over the edge of the precipice but, like Ghadar, Lalaynia stood her ground. The captor shouted for help from the nearest of his men who was ripping at the packs on Ghadar's back, looking for treasures he could steal.

The dark, leering faces of the attackers seemed to swim all around Michael and his horses. Two evil warriors tugged and struck at Lalaynia. Another tried to pull Michael from her back, while two others ripped what was left of the packs off of Ghadar. Still fighting off his own attackers, Michael watched in horror as two of the others tried to send Ghadar over the cliff.

All at once, recalling the angelic protectors his logical young mind usually dismissed, he called out. "If you're near, we could use some help!"

No sooner had he asked, than from out of nowhere came a great wind, accompanied by a horrible wailing sound that seemed to intensify the awful force of the gale. The marauders began to scatter, their eyes glazed with fear, their arms flailing as if to ward off invisible blows. But in the small space occupied by Michael and his horses, the air was calm and still. The three companions could only watch as every member of the demonic band was blown into oblivion, disappearing as fast as they had materialized.

Michael's goods lay scattered about on the trail, only a few things having fallen down the steep mountainside.

The packs were torn in places, but not beyond repair. With trembling hands, the boy repacked and secured the baggage on Ghadar's back, and the trio resumed their descent into the valley below.

In its aftermath, the encounter seemed almost surreal. But given the damage, there was no way to deny its authenticity. Above all, his deliverance proved to the boy that he was again Divinely protected.

"Are You there, then?" Michael whispered into the descending night as the travelers looked for a place to rest. "If You really do exist, as my father believed, will You one day bring us together again?" It was a question that would remain, for a time, unanswered. But at least this young man had finally asked it.

As the days and nights advanced uneventfully, the adventurers settled back into their easy routine, with Lalaynia still choosing the route. As though they had passed some frightful test, there were no more attacks.

Once or twice Michael saw groups of riders off in the distance, but no one again accosted them. With a new faith that began to mature following their deliverance, Michael had started to pray for protection, offering up a steady liturgy as he rode along. For him, the One God was at last real and worthy of trust.

They had been following the Euphrates for some time when the mare stopped and gazed off toward the western horizon, for the first time appearing to be undecided. The plain that spread to the west looked desolate and fearsome, whereas to the north the land remained friendly.

"Let's stay with the river," Michael said, stroking Lalaynia's mane. But the mare shook her lovely head and dropped her nose into the grass where she began eating as though it was time to stop for the night. Since the sun was beginning its slow descent after the peak of its day, Michael decided to make camp beside the Euphrates and to contemplate the predicament that seemed now to present itself.

"Which way do we go?" he asked the breeze, hoping the One God would hear and, uncharacteristically, settling in to await His answer.

It was cool beneath the trees that grew up along the river banks. When he had satisfied his hunger and his thirst, Michael lay down for a little nap. "I'll know what to do when I awaken," he told himself, closing his eyes and surrendering to the drowsiness that engulfed him. Nearby, Lalaynia and Ghadar grazed on the lush river grass, peaceful, but fully alert in case any danger might threaten.

Michael awoke to snorts from Ghadar and nudging from Lalaynia. While he slept, the night sky had descended, edging out the day. Somehow the darkness confused and disoriented him, and he felt a nagging twinge of fear. Now Lalaynia became insistent, nickering as she pushed her soft nose into Michael's middle, as if trying to get him on his feet.

"What do you want?" Michael asked. "We can't travel now. It's dark and we'll lose our way."

But the mare wouldn't be put off, so finally the boy stood up and went with the horses to the edge of the little copse of trees under which they had rested, following their gaze across the plain. The sight Michael beheld took his breath away. Off in the far distance, rising up out of the horizon, was a Star of such indefinable brilliance that the sight of it made him stagger back a step and shield his still sleepy eyes.

Shaped like no other the boy had ever seen, the Celestial Body seemed to throb with life, not twinkling as did its smaller heavenly companions, but surging with a power that was almost tangible. It was as though the tail of the Star pointed toward some unknown treasure beneath it, and all at once Michael felt like he was being awakened from a deep sleep. This, he knew, was the Star that had been foretold as the beacon that would guide the Magi to the Baby King.

Look for me when you see the Star that heralds the birth of the Savior.

Archanus' last words to his son now rang joyfully in Michael's ears. Never mind that Archanus had not been chosen for the Magi's mission. Michael would not abandon the hope that his father would find a way to follow his long-held dream.

As if she too recalled Archanus' words, Lalaynia pressed against Michael, insisting he pay attention.

Reaching around to her own side, she grabbed between her teeth the blanket that lay across her back, then began to nibble at the boy's shirt.

"Do you want me to get on your back?" Michael asked. Bumping her pretty nose forward once, twice, three times, the mare seemed to answer, "Yes."

"All right then." Michael laughed. "Have it your way."

That night the companions covered more ground than ever before in the same period of time. Lalaynia and Ghadar loped tirelessly across the rolling dunes of sand as though their hooves never really touched the ground. The Star mysteriously drew these travelers toward it, giving them the freedom of winged creatures and strength beyond imagining.

The comrades should have been exhausted as the dawn approached. They should have been scorched by the relentless desert heat as the sun made its inexorable ascent from the eastern horizon. But even the sun's dominance was eclipsed as it raced across the sky toward the Star, whose preeminence remained unchallenged.

They should have been hungry and thirsty as the day wore into night. But they were none of these things. For a time the travelers were immortal, carried on wings of angels toward a destiny Michael accepted without question, though he could not fully comprehend its extraordinary importance.

CHAPTER
Twelve

As night gathered on the fourth day of this miraculous odyssey, Michael recognized the sounds and the smells of a place where people erected permanent structures and lived within too close proximity of one another. Even had this boy not spent a good share of his life in nomadic freedom, he would have found repugnant such clustering together of humanity. The liberty of the broad spaces which had been his home merely served to heighten his senses and elevate the disdain with which he viewed such settlements.

Still, Michael felt himself being drawn toward the heart of the city called Bethlehem. At any other time, he would have made his way quietly around a permanent encampment of this sort, being careful not to expose himself to its inhabitants unless they were familiar suppliers of goods to his family. But not tonight. Tonight he was drawn on toward that place beneath the tail of the Star where the Angel of Destiny awaited him.

No one confronted the boy and his horses as they made their way through the narrow streets of the settlement. His sensitivity heightened by the angelic army who traveled with him, Michael was able to hear the conversations whispered behind the closed doors of the houses. Moreover, the One God made it possible for the traveler to understand the varied and unfamiliar languages and to recognize the uneasiness of the people who spoke.

Residents talked of the census being taken. Those who had traveled to the city in obedience to the Roman edict were anxious to be counted and to return to their homes. All were afraid this census was nothing more than an exercise of Roman power and almost certainly a harbinger of greater oppression and higher taxes.

Every discussion, whether by townspeople or visitors, eventually came to the Star. To those who did not understand its portent, the appearance of the enormous light was a frightening event.

Listening carefully, Michael learned much. For quite some time it had been impossible for anyone residing in, or traveling around, this area to ignore the approach, and finally the all pervading Presence of this Celestial Body. When the Star first appeared on the distant eastern horizon, it was only slightly larger and brighter than were its companions in the night sky. Then it had begun to move across the heavens.

As it traveled westward, it grew brighter and more concentrated until it reached this place where it at last came to rest. Now the Star's dazzling brilliance put an end to the darkness of night. All this, the people could observe, if not understand. What they could not, then, see or know was that the light from the great Star symbolized the Illumination that would come to the world through the One whose birth it heralded.

Although Michael sensed the fear and confusion of the people who huddled behind Bethlehem's closed doors, he would not acknowledge his own apprehension. He knew he must make his way to the place marked by the Star. He did not know what would happen when he arrived. He hoped he would find his father waiting there. But all at once his passion for the reunion was mysteriously overshadowed by something more—an emotion too immense for his comprehension.

In his heart, if not yet in his mind, the young horseman understood that he was approaching the Nativity . . . the Birth of the Christ . . . the arrival of the Savior Archanus had anticipated with such great hope. In these moments of mystical clarity, a powerful awareness he had never felt before carried Michael forward. Lalaynia and Ghadar, too, seemed to perceive the nearness of their goal, as well as the urgency and the need for quiet. Without a snort or a nicker they proceeded, the sound of their hooves strangely muted as they moved silently across the hard-packed streets.

When they at last reached their destination, all was still—and yet, the night pulsed with a profound vitality. The palpable silence was at once resonant and harmonious. Darkness did not exist, and yet there were no shadows. The atmosphere shimmered like liquid gold, but its density clarified rather than diffused the scene. The air vibrated with power, and the entire region was suffused with the almost tangible Presence of Holiness.

His entire being captivated by the immense Authority that surrounded him, Michael slipped down from Lalaynia's back. Dropping to his knees in humility, he worshipped openly and without shame. His heart and his mind overflowing with the enormity of the moment, Michael's words tumbled over one another.

"Thank You . . . Thank You," the boy whispered. "But, how can this be? How can I have been thus chosen? Is my father here? Will he yet arrive? He has to be here, or why should I have come? Surely You would not allow me to see this Miracle if You did not also bring my father who has sought this moment always . . ."

As he continued to murmur words of praise, Michael was transported beyond the moment into the silence of his soul where his heart and mind were at last stilled by an exquisite peace that flowed around and through him. A soft sigh escaped his parted lips as he allowed himself to be filled with the elemental knowledge of the Child's Sovereign Deity, a perfect assurance that supplanted all else in his logical, young mind.

At peace, Michael, still kneeling, raised his eyes to survey the scene before him. Only now that the outpouring of his heart was complete, could he begin to comprehend the setting of the Miracle.

Before him, a man and a woman clad in plain peasant garments knelt beside a manger that rested within a natural shelter carved out of the rocky hillside. Normally a refuge that protected farm animals from the elements, the little haven pulsed now with the wonder of new life. A cow lay peacefully not far behind the woman. Nearby, a goat nibbled on the straw that covered the ground of the alcove and the surrounding stable yard. Now and then a small, burrowing creature would peek out to survey the scene. A covey of chickens and a lone dove roosted in the eves of the cavern. Just outside, to the west of the humble sanctuary, a family of shepherds tended their flock. Silently observing something they could not begin to comprehend, the men stood guard while their sheep rested for the night.

On the east side of the shelter, three Magi, garbed in the finery of Oriental kings, knelt, facing the manger. Their heads bowed in reverent prayer, their hands clasped before them, their voices were barely audible as they gave thanks to the One God for the greatest Gift the world would ever know. Behind the Magi their camels rested, their saddle packs still laden with the gifts these first worshippers of the Christ had brought to honor the Child they knew to be the Son of the One God.

Michael recognized Balthazar at once, but the other two Wise Men's faces were obscured. At the sight of these men, both of whom were large in stature like his father, Michael's heart swelled with hope. In any other circumstance, the boy would have rushed forward to look in the Magi's faces. But not tonight. Though his whole being ached with longing, he was captivated and stilled by a reverence more compelling than anything he had ever felt.

The sweet smell of dried grasses and warm animal bodies wafted across the night on a gentle breeze. The pungent steam of animal dung mingled with the honeyed breaths of the assembled creatures and drifted into the stable, warming the shelter for the Holy Family. For an immeasurable distance of time, no human, no creature, stirred. The cow and the camels ceased their endless chewing. The goat stopped nibbling at the straw. The sheep huddled together, perfectly still. The gentle sounds of the chickens and the dove were silenced. The horses neither blinked an eye nor twitched an ear. And the peace of the prolonged interval enveloped the little assembly.

Then, all at once, in response to the Child's distinct though wordless bidding, Lalaynia, beside whom Michael still knelt, took a tentative step forward. The Baby's Mother nodded her head, almost imperceptibly, encouraging the mare to come forward. Her own head low in supplication, Lalaynia moved calmly toward the Family. Still, no one spoke, no other creature moved. At last Lalaynia stretched her neck so that her soft muzzle touched the tiny hand that extended toward her.

Since his arrival, Michael had been able to see the Baby lying in the little feed trough. Yet only now, did he perceive the intense radiance that emanated from the Child. A fleeting thought that he should pull Lalaynia away passed briefly across Michael's mind, but the idea disappeared as quickly as it had come. Instead, all he could do was watch in stunned silence as an event took place that he would never be able to adequately describe.

At the Child's Touch, Lalaynia was surrounded by a lucent, almost material gleam that swelled and vibrated with power. The song of the night soared into a symphony of praise. And through it all, the mare stood placidly, her soft, dark eyes half-closed, her muzzle resting against the upturned palm of the Christ Child.

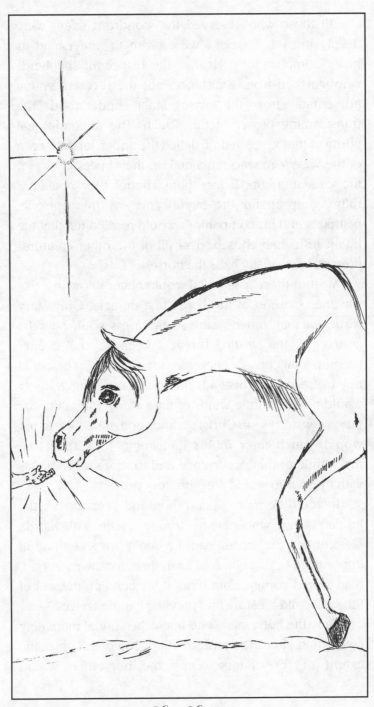

All those who observed the wondrous event were deeply moved. Yet none were given to understand its historic implications. Neither the respectful shepherds who watched from a distance, nor the reverent young horseman, nor the wise Magi understood the transforming power of this Touch. The unconditional purity of that space in time defied the understanding even of the Wise Men who remained on their knees in awe of the scene unfolding before them. Though they would not fully comprehend the significance of this episode, Balthazar and his companions would recall often that the Infant Jesus had chosen, over all of the other creatures present, to specially bless the horse.

Most of those assembled would never know that this was the occasion of the Lord's first miracle. Only Mary suspected that somehow this single caress would alter the course of the world, forever. Because the event's monumental consequence was not understood, it would not be recorded. Instead, this portion of the Nativity would be lost on the winds of time along with all of the other mysteries of Christ's childhood. Michael alone would, much later in his life, begin to suspect the magnitude of that occurrence and to share his thoughts with those who would pass the story on.

It would be more than a thousand years before the human beings, who were the true recipients of the Lord's Blessing of the horse, would begin to feel the full importance of that gift. And even then, for the most part, man would congratulate himself for bending the will of this once wild creature and pressing it into service.

Only the horsemen, who knew the animal intimately before and after the transformation, could recognize the extent of the change. Only the horsemen would understand that the Blessing placed within the hearts of every descendant of Lalaynia's the desire to serve its human companions. Unbeknownst to Michael, you see, Lalaynia had conceived before their departure and was, even then, carrying a magnificent horse-colt. Only the horsemen would, much later, recognize the fact that the Blessing bestowed upon Lalaynia's son would ultimately enable humankind to connect, to cultivate, and to civilize God's once vastly segregated world.

In the wake of the Blessing, another was given, and oh so gratefully received. Silent tears coursed down the cheeks of the still kneeling Michael as suddenly he was overcome by the knowledge that he had witnessed an enormous event—a great wonder which his father had not been allowed to share. Now the pain in the boy's heart called out to the Sacred Heart of the Child who lay before him.

As He had beckoned the mare, the Christ Child silently invited Michael to come nearer. Hesitantly, the young horseman stepped forward, his trembling hand reaching toward the Babe. At the will of Jesus, Michael tenderly grasped the Child's outstretched hand, and the eyes of the Messiah met those of His youthful servant. The same brilliance the Christ had cast around Lalaynia, now surrounded Michael. Once more, time was suspended, and in the stillness, the Infant Jesus rekindled Michael's faith, filling the young man's entire being with an indelible message of hope and love.

As though Archanus were right beside him, Michael heard once more his father's parting assurance. *It is promised that we will be reunited. We must hold on to this knowledge, and to our love for the One God, and one another. No matter what happens in the years ahead, no matter how long it takes, we must chart our varied courses by the Star of Faith that will one day guide us back to one another. We cannot succumb to fear or disillusionment. We must believe.*

With those words, the Christ Child gave Michael the gifts of faith, hope, and love that would forever surpass all understanding—treasures that would fortify the young adventurer for all that lay before him. The fears, the dangers, the sorrows of a lifetime, no matter how monumental, would always pale in the reflected light of these Gifts which, like the Blessing of the horse, the Lord offered that day to all of humankind.

There is no way to know how long God suspended time for those He had brought to this zenith in history. We are only privy to the fact that after some indeterminate period, the Star began to recede into the west. The shepherds returned to their wandering. The Magi, accompanied by Michael, set off on a journey in search of Archanus, who was not, after all, among those present. And the Holy Family blended, for a short while, into the safe anonymity of their surroundings.

In the book we now call the *Bible*, it is said that the Magi returned to their country by another route. According to *The Lost Legend,* this statement is symbolic of far more than the obvious. It is said that the Wise Men's journeys were forever altered by the Divine Providence that made them witness to the Birth of the Savior. From that day forward, the sect known as the Magi disappeared from history.

Could it be, as *The Legend* tells us, that the Magi, in fact, became the very first disciples of Christ? Could these keepers of wisdom, as those who passed on *The Legend* believed, never have been heard from again because they became students of His ancestry and then followers of His teachings? Is this so difficult to imagine? Is there a simple answer to this question? Only the One God knows.

And Michael? What would become of him? And what of Lalaynia and Ghadar? What could be left for a boy so young who had been priviledged to witness the Nativity of the Christ and to share in the greatest story ever told?

While Gaspar and Melchior, the two Wise Men who had accompanied Balthazar, prepared for their departure, the third Magi approached Michael.

"We must talk." The Magi's voice was deep and gentle as he reached out and placed a hand on Michael's shoulder.

One hand still resting on Ghadar's withers, Michael turned and was oddly captivated by the old king. Surveying the Wise Man, Michael wondered why he had never noticed before that Balthazar's eyes, like his own and those of his mother, were the rare and extraordinary light blue that often frightened their dark-eyed kinsmen.

"The eyes are the mirror of the soul," Junia had taught him long ago. "Be it horse or human, this feature exposes the good or the evil of the spirit within." Now, that which lived within Balthazar was revealed to Michael through the mirror of the Wise Man's soul.

There was a chill in the morning air, but the bareheaded Balthazar showed no sign of discomfort. Thick, white hair covered his head and a full, white beard graced his smiling face. Everything about this man spoke to Michael of family and safety and permanence.

"I know not why I have been given this information," Balthazar said, his hand still resting lightly on Michael's shoulder. "I only know that I am to tell you that a great commission still lies ahead of you—a sacred trust not yet revealed."

"What does this mean? Where am I to go to learn of this assignment?" Michael asked, unconsciosly grasping the talisman that hung around his neck.

"I do not know," answered Balthazar. "I can only assume that all will be revealed to you in due course."

"Where will your travels take you?"

Looking squarely at the boy and making no move to leave, Balthazar answered. "We go in search of the man who was to have led us on this mission. Though relatively young, he was the wisest and most learned of our sect, and until recently we thought him lost."

"Do you know who I am?"

"Yes," answered Balthazar. "I have known since I saw you at the horseman's camp."

"Why did you not speak of your knowledge then?"

"It was obvious that your mother's brother, John, felt he must keep your identity a secret. He could not have known that I could be trusted. And I, myself, was unsure of the men who accompanied me on that journey."

The sounds and smells of the morning filled the stable yard outside the little alcove wherein the Holy Family still resided. As the cold light of dawn gave way to the warming sun, the young horseman and the elder Magi held one another's gazes, their minds linked in thought, their hearts connected by Christ's all powerful love.

"You know that I must go with you now."

"Yes, I suppose I do." Balthazar's answer was tentative.

"But you do not approve of this choice?"

"It is not for me to judge," the Wise Man countered, "though somehow it does not seem the right decision."

"How can it be wrong?" Michael pleaded. "The One God has brought us together. This must mean that He is at last leading me to my father."

"Perhaps . . ." There was still uncertainty in Balthazar's reply. Then, his blue eyes lit up with renewed passion as he recalled the Blessing bestowed upon Michael by the Infant Jesus. "You must hold fast to the faith imparted to you when you were touched by the Messiah. Whatever the One God has in store for you, this Great Blessing will sustain and strenghten you."

Not wanting to be left behind and hoping to avoid debate, Michael rushed on. "How will we find my father?" he asked. "Where will our search begin?"

"He has been seen in the company of a respected Greek physician named Luke. We will go to that country north of the Great Sea where these companions are said to be carrying out the work assigned them by the One God."

"Then it's settled. I will ride with you," Michael said hopefully, the hint of a question revealing his uncertainty. "We should cross paths with my mother's people before too long. We can procure new mounts for us all. The horses will make the journey much faster . . ."

"Aren't you getting a bit ahead of yourself?" Balthazar's patient response was unnerving.

"I'm sorry," Michael said. "It's just that I've waited so long to find my father . . . and I feel your disapproval. Please, tell me, why do you not want me to go with you?"

"It's not that I don't want you," Balthazar said, "and there's no need for you to apologize. I understand your great desire for reunion with your father. There is nothing I would like better than to share with you this quest. I just have this sense that your mission here has not been completed and that riding away with us is not the One God's plan for you."

The entreaty in Michael's eyes was more than the old man could bear. "Never mind me." Balthazar sighed and wrapped a surprisingly strong arm around Michael. "You will accompany us. But please, do not be too surprised or disappointed if things don't work out exactly as you expect them to."

"I can't worry about that now," Michael said, a smile returning to his handsome face as his hopes of finding his father once more overshadowed all else.

When the travelers tried to take their leave, Lalaynia and Ghadar exhibited their displeasure without restraint. Never had Michael been faced with such difficult behavior by the horses, and never had he been less sensitive to their higher instincts. Finally, following a prolonged battle of wills, Michael appeared to triumph and the companions began their new journey.

Not so far down the road, Michael's new found faith and willingness to obey the One God would be sorely tested when an angel of the Lord would appear and call him to return to Jerusalem.

"The Child and His earthly parents are in grave danger. And you have been chosen to escort them out of harm's way."

But then, that's another story . . .

EPILOGUE
Epilogue

The storyteller would not be worthy of this tale if no effort were made to explain the momentous consequences of the Miracle.

To fully understand the magnitude of Christ's Blessing of the horse, one must first recognize certain essential truths relative to this animal. To begin with, this is a creature so large, so mighty, that there is virtually no reason for it to cooperate with mankind unless God ordained that it should do so.

Further, one must know that for several thousand years the horse was available to none but the wealthy and the powerful. Most historians would have us believe that the only limiting factor in this circumstance was money. But there was more to it than that.

The horse was an animal of extraordinary strength and resistance, with no natural affinity for mankind. The arrogant and strong of will had no conscience about the use of force in the subduing of animals, or of those humans they considered less important than themselves. Some early horses succumbed to the overweening power of their tormentors. Some escaped. Some perished in the battle of wills. The most fortunate were cherished and trained by such horsemen as those of Junia's family. But none were easily bent to the volition of man . . . until the Blessing.

With no more than a touch of His hand, the Son of God changed the course of history for all time when He placed in the heart of Lalaynia, and all the horses that would descend from her, the simple desire to serve humankind.

It happened, you see, that the colt Lalaynia carried on that prodigious occasion of her Blessing would found a dynasty. From this line would come the most beautiful, tractable, intelligent horses the world would ever know. Again, that's another story.

Suffice it now to say that, in time, the precious blood of Lalaynia, through her son, Zabbai, would infiltrate those fine herds under the protection of the chosen horsemen. It would take many generations for this legacy to extend throughout the world, but ultimately the horse would cease to resist man. Eventually these noble creatures would peacefully serve the humble, the gentle, the meek. No longer would access to the horse be the singular privilege of the forceful and the affluent. One day, good people, even those who did not share the horsemen's understanding and knowledge, would become partners with the horse in the advancement of civilization.

Biblical history supports a significant change relative to the horse, following the birth of Christ. Old Testament prophets regarded the horse as a fearsome creature, a threat, a symbol of oppression and mankind's disregard for God's laws. Later, in the Book of Revelation (the final book of the New Testament) St. John has a glorious vision of the Lord and His army returning on white horses to finally save the world.

Why, though, did God choose the horse over all the other animals of His creation? We can only speculate. Perhaps this handsome creature always held a special place in the heart of the One God. Maybe, from the very beginning, the horse was specially designed by God to carry out the tasks for which this animal is so uniquely suited. What other, after all, has such great heart, such courage? What other is so perfectly constructed for the comfort of the rider? What other animal, large enough to be ridden by humans, can cover ground with such speed? What other species, strong enough to pull and carry great loads, can be harnessed to work in tandem or with a team for greatest efficiency?

Whatever His reasons, the Lord chose the horse. But what did this animal do that was so important? That's the simple part of this story. We have merely to look back across the centuries to find the answer. At the time when Christ was born, the communities and countries of the world were isolated by distance. A trek of 100 miles was almost unthinkable for those who had only their two legs for conveyance. In that day, farming was a painstaking process. Small plots of ground were sowed and reaped primarily by the work of human hands, and the results were limited at best.

When the horse became man's servant, everything changed. Travel became easier and faster. People of diverse background and environment became familiar with and were enriched by one another.

Previously unsettled lands were colonized and developed. In short, it can truly be said that the inhabitants of the earth were connected by horsepower.

The land was cultivated by horsepower. The vast and varied cultures were civilized by horsepower. God made all of this possible through His gift to humankind of a miraculous partnership with the horse.

Modern historians commonly mark time by citing world changing eras. Among those periods are such epochs as the Bronze Age, when new tools and weapons made it easier for man to acquire food and to begin tilling the land.

Then came the Iron Age, when this stronger, more resilient material improved man's bronze equipment. Later there was the Industrial Age, when all manner of goods were made more readily available through manufacturing. And, most recently, the Age of Technology and Electronics which has intensified the speed and efficacy of communication and taken progress into another, somewhat frightening, dimension.

For some reason, though, the Age of the Horse, and the awesome changes brought about by this season in time, are most often overlooked. That interval, which entered its initial phase with the first generation born of Lalaynia's son, continued well into the 20th Century. The results, felt around the globe as lands were cultivated and wars were won—largely because of the horse—were far more monumental than the effects of any other of those periods so regularly heralded for their great contributions to world progress. The plain truth is that without the horse, an unquestionable gift from God, civilization as we know it today would not exist.

In light of this knowledge, we must never forget that with His Gift of the horse, God charged the animals' human caretakers with a most awesome responsibility. When we were enabled to remove the horse from its natural habitat, we became bound to provide for it. When we were granted the horse's willingness to serve us, we became obligated to treat it with fairness, asking of the creature only that which we honestly needed from it.

Through the horse, God gave mankind a very special form of liberty, a bequest which altered not only the face of the earth, but the heart and spirit of its human inhabitants. To diminish that gift or to ignore the unparalleled trust it represents is a sin against the Giver.

With this book, and the ones that will follow, I offer my own heartfelt thanks to our Creator for His gift to me, and to you, of the horse.

Watch for Book Two of
THE LOST LEGEND TRILOGY
Scheduled for Release
in the Fall of 2000
If you would like to be on the mailing list
for advance notice, please drop us a note
at the below address or fax number.

If you enjoyed
THE LOST LEGEND OF THE FIRST CHRISTMAS
and are unable to
obtain additional copies from
your local bookstore, (in 1999 or 2000)
you can order directly from:

AMPELOS PRESS
Colorado Office • P.O. Box 773632
Steamboat Springs, Colorado 80477
Call Toll Free: 888-79-HORSE (794-6773)
Fax Toll Free: 888-294-6337
www.horses-online.com/horselegend
Master Card and Visa Accepted
Discounts available for large quantity orders